LETHAL MISCONDUCT

8/19

Help us Rate this book...
Put your initials on the
Left side and your rating
on the right side.
1 = Didn't care for
2 = It was O.K.
3 = It was great

	DATE DUE		
AUG 2 6 2018			
DEC 0 6 2019			
DEC 2 7 2019			

MRH	1 2 3			
	1 2 3			
	1 2 3			
	1 2 3			
	1 2 3			
	1 2 3			
	1 2 3			
	1 2 3			
	1 2 3			
	1 2 3			
	1 2 3			
	1 2 3			
	1 2 3			
	1 2 3			
	1 2 3			PRINTED IN U.S.A.

LETHAL MISCONDUCT

Book 6 of the Corps Justice Series
Copyright © 2014, 2018 C. G. Cooper Entertainment. All
Rights Reserved
Author: C. G. Cooper

GET A FREE COPY OF THE CORPS JUSTICE PREQUEL SHORT STORY, *GOD-SPEED*, JUST FOR SUBSCRIBING AT CG-COOPER.COM

CORPS JUSTICE

Corps Justice Oath by Col. Calvin Stokes, Sr. (USMC, Ret.)

1. We will protect and defend the Constitution of the United States.

2. We will protect the weak and punish the wicked.

3. When the laws of this nation hinder the completion of these duties, our moral compass will guide us to see the mission through.

———

Si Vis Pacem, Para Iustitiam: In order to have peace, you must first have justice.

NORTH FLORIDA REGIONAL MEDICAL CENTER

GAINESVILLE, FLORIDA - 7:00AM, APRIL 6TH

He walked with a practiced air, looking perfectly at home in his blue scrubs and well-worn camouflage patterned scrub cap. The hospital staff was too busy with morning turnover and rounds to notice him. Besides, he looked like any number of surgeons: trim, serious, all business.

It wasn't hard getting into the more secure halls of the hospital. He'd been in too many to count and knew the level of deference given to physicians. He was a doctor, after all, just not one who was currently affiliated with any facility in the United States. It wasn't impossible that someone would stop him, but it had only happened once in his travels. In the end, he'd reluctantly aborted that mission, feigning embarrassment and slinking away.

Finding patients was the easy part. Selecting the right one was tricky considering his dwindling supply. Success was paramount. What he wouldn't give for access to his old lab. But that wasn't going to happen.

He ignored the bored look of a sleepy nurse and grabbed a chart from a metal rack. It wasn't his first trip into the ward. He'd had to find his target beforehand, had to make sure the patient fit the profile. Failure would not be tolerated. He wouldn't allow it.

Examining the chart as he walked, the intruder scanned the notes, confirming his own determination. Diagnosed weeks earlier. Cancer. Terminal. According to her physician's scribbled remarks, she'd been told, but didn't believe she was dying.

He opened the door to Room 307 after knocking lightly.

"Hello?" The sleepy voice from inside was accompanied by the slight creaking of the hospital bed.

The doctor switched on the light, inhaling the smell he'd come to associate with impending death. Antiseptic and a forced cleanliness that were somehow supposed to mask the odor of the dying.

"How are you feeling this morning, Mrs. Miller?" he asked, still studying the chart, careful not to make direct eye contact.

"Better, Doctor. I really think the radiation is working." Mrs. Miller squinted. "I'm sorry, are you one of my doctors?"

"Not really. Doctor Peterson is an old friend. He wanted me to stop by and have a look at your progress. Just trying to go the extra mile. Came down from Mayo this morning." He'd been amazed at how well the use of The Mayo's Clinic's name perked people up.

Mrs. Miller nodded, relaxing. "That's very kind of you, Doctor."

"It's my pleasure, Mrs. Miller. Now, feel free to get back to sleep if you'd like. I'm just going to do a quick check on all these beeping things over here and then I'll get out of your hair."

Mrs. Miller smiled sleepily, her once round face now tightening around her cheekbones. According to her records, she'd already lost sixty pounds.

Turning away from the patient, the doctor pretended to be checking the array of monitors behind the bed. Once he knew Mrs. Miller was no longer looking, he slipped a capped syringe out of his pants pocket. It took less than ten seconds to inject the solution into the IV line that was providing Mrs. Miller with a slow drip of saline and electrolytes.

He recapped the syringe and replaced it in his pocket, stepping around the bed to look down on the patient. Like every time before, he swore there was already a visible change, but he knew intuitively that it would take days for the drug to run its course.

Patting the resting woman on her hand, he said, "Hope you feel better soon, Mrs. Miller."

She nodded with closed eyes and drifted off to sleep as he slipped out the door, now hurrying to leave, his guard up. This was the trickiest part, mostly because his adrenaline raced. He'd been careful to avoid the video cameras, opting for a circuitous route to the ICU.

Not five minutes later, Dr. Hunter Price stepped out of the service exit, the smell of rotting vegetables hitting him from the dumpster sitting askew against the brick wall next to the door. Glancing around, he grabbed the backpack he'd stashed behind the garbage, quickly slipping on a pair of track pants and a windbreaker and stuffing his scrub cap in the bag in exchange for the white Nike running visor.

Price slung the backpack over one shoulder and headed toward the bus stop, knowing he was cutting it close before the next one arrived. As he stepped to cross the street, still keeping his eyes downcast, he heard a car door shut. Looking up as casually as he could, his gaze locked onto the man standing next to a forest green Ford F-150, his arm resting on the side of the truck bed. He wore a pair of black wraparound sunglasses despite the overcast day. His dark suit and tie made him look like a Secret Service agent, only with an added hint of menace that seemed to radiate from the man's placid demeanor.

Dr. Price increased his speed, noticing the man walking in pursuit, stalking like a panther. There was fifty yards to go to the bus stop where three nurses stood chatting and puffing away on cigarettes. To his left Price heard the revving of a large engine. The bus was coming.

He could feel the man behind him, closing the gap with his longer strides. How had they found him? He'd been careful, more so than in months past. And yet...

The bus came to a halt and opened its doors for the waiting passengers, who hastily took their last drags before throwing the still burning cigs on the ground. He was fifty feet from the bus, forty. He waved to the bus driver who motioned for him to hurry up.

He broke into a jog, thankful for the impatient public servant staring at him in annoyance. Dr. Price hopped aboard the bus, handing over his prepaid bus pass, glancing furtively behind him.

"That guy with you?" asked the driver, pointing.

"No, uh, he works for my wife's lawyer. Trying to serve me papers. Can you step on it?"

The overweight bus driver took a split second to make his decision, closing the doors with a hiss and stepping on the gas just as the man in sunglasses reached to knock on the door.

Dr. Hunter Price breathed a sigh of relief. "Thanks."

"No problem. Just went through a nasty divorce last year. I fucking hate lawyers."

Price nodded and watched as his shadow passed far

behind, still staring at the bus like a statue. Menacing as always.

Dr. Price took a seat, his legs shaking, trying to figure out how he could avoid being found in the future. Then again, if he didn't find a way to replenish his supplies, it wouldn't matter.

CHARLOTTESVILLE, VIRGINIA

9:34AM, APRIL 4TH

Cal Stokes took his time walking down the busy sidewalk that skirted Rugby Road, or what might be called 'Fraternity Row.' He was heading against the masses, University of Virginia students making their way to class on the brilliant spring day, the sun casting a welcome glow on its travelers.

The harsh winter had gratefully ended, spring now full on as the end of the semester loomed. There was an excitement in the air. He could feel it.

Cal remembered his days at U.Va fondly. He'd never graduated, instead opting to enlist in the Marine Corps after his parents' death on 9/11, but he'd come full circle. There might be time to finish his degree later, should he choose that course, but the former Marine's schedule was full. He allowed himself one walk down memory lane each morning, today it was a stroll down to the Corner, the University's retail hub, for a ham, egg and cheese bagel at Bodo's.

As Cal dodged another cute co-ed who blushed a silent

sorry as she almost collided with him, he thought about the last month and the changes he'd endured. First, his cousin Travis Haden, once the CEO of Stokes Security International (SSI), the company Cal's father had founded, accepted the invitation of President Brandon Zimmer to become his chief of staff. There'd been a moment where Cal almost slid into the CEO role at SSI, what with being the sole owner and all, but that hadn't sat well with Cal. He was a warrior, not a paper pusher.

Instead, he'd come up with the brilliant idea of recommending that the company's only female employee, Marge "The Hammer" Haines, a powerful lawyer with the beauty and lethality of a black widow, take over as head of his company. It hadn't taken long for him to regret that decision.

The honeymoon barely lasted two weeks, ending with Marge informing Cal that it was time for him to leave SSI, permanently. At the time, he'd been enraged, storming out like a child, disappearing for days, out of contact despite numerous phone calls from his closest friends.

The time away had given him room to think. Over the years SSI had developed a highly effective covert division that took the battle to the enemy. It was Cal's team and he loved it like a father loves his first child. Cal and his team zealously jumped into fights that government agencies and local law enforcement couldn't wage. Their focus was the heart of America, the core of their beloved country. While the public divisions of SSI provided security for the government and VIPs overseas and developed groundbreaking new technology, courtesy of Cal's best friend Neil Patel, Cal's boys stayed in the shadows, killing when needed, crippling threats as they appeared.

But that was over. While Cal hated to admit it, Marge was right. There'd been more than one instance when they'd almost been discovered. The resulting fall-out would have crippled SSI and likely cost their employees their jobs. Separating the two was inevitable. It had just taken Cal a few days to get to the same conclusion.

What Cal hadn't known until he'd shown his face back at Camp Spartan, SSI's primary headquarters just outside Nashville, TN, was that President Zimmer had been part of Marge's decision. He'd floated the idea that perhaps a new organization be established. One that could disappear if needed and yet be powerful enough to handle delicate operations on and off U.S. soil. Specifically, the president needed a group he could rely on that wasn't handcuffed by the increasingly noose-tight regulations of the law. He needed someone he could trust. He needed Cal Stokes.

Cal and the president hadn't been mutual admirers from the start. What with the former congressman being a Massachusetts Democrat and Cal a conservative Marine, their initial introduction was tumultuous at best. But that had changed. Through the duplicity of Zimmer's now deceased father, Senator Richard Zimmer, and multiple attempts on Brandon's life, Cal had been there for his friend. They'd forged a bond through fire and lead. Now, despite their political differences, the two held each other in high regard.

The president's idea had first come as a surprise to Cal, who was still reeling from the shock of being dismissed from his own company. But without much prompting, the stubborn Marine came to see the merits of Zimmer's proposal. He would have complete autonomy, as long as they didn't get caught.

So while the split from SSI still stung, Cal was getting used to his new role. The first thing the president had suggested when Cal said yes was for Cal to reach out to a billionaire entrepreneur named Jonas Layton. Jonas had been one of the key pieces in an operation the previous month when the secretary of state was implicated in a complex scheme involving the Russians trying to collapse the U.S. stock market. The threat had been dealt with and Cal and Jonas departed friends.

What the president had in mind worked to perfection. Jonas, who was known as "The Fortuneteller" by most of the tech world for his prognosticative skills, would be the face of the new organization. Because he had plenty of money, the young billionaire would front the start-up capital, and any outlays not recouped through investing would be reimbursed by one of the president's discretionary funds. Jonas hadn't flinched, already bored despite his constant traveling.

Cal had two requests. The first was that he be allowed to choose the location of the new headquarters. He'd picked Charlottesville both for his love of the area and its proximity to Washington, D.C. The president and Jonas agreed and within days Cal had purchased a home just off of the University's popular Fraternity Row on Rugby Road.

His second request was that he be allowed to bring on anyone he wanted. Again, the president didn't object.

They were still finalizing their official cover, but were in no rush to do so. Jonas had been the first to craft his story, securing a visiting professorship at U.Va within the McIntire School of Commerce. The dean, an old friend from their days in Silicon Valley, had readily accepted the offer, and Professor Jonas Layton's fall class was already the talk of school. Enrollment would fill in seconds.

The crowd had thinned by the time Cal neared the intersection where Rugby Road continued at a sharp left and Preston Avenue went right. They'd purchased one of the properties on the corner and were in the process of negotiating with the owner across the street for another. With just under two acres on their new property and about 4,500 square feet of living space, the growing team could make do

for the time being. They really needed to double the space –
hence the purchase of the second property.

Jonas had money to spend and didn't mind splurging a
little bit on real estate. He'd already offered the second home-
owner well above what he could make on the open market.
Jonas said it was just a matter of time. Cal believed him. He'd
come to understand that the billionaire didn't let much stand
in his way. Jonas would fit right in with the determined group
of warriors now taking up residence in the heart of Charlottesville.

Cal turned left onto the path that was more dirt than
grass, the current back entrance to the property. It would
soon be walled off with the latest security equipment
designed by none other than the tech genius Neil Patel,
himself also a University of Virginia alum.

The parcel of land was shaped in a rough pentagon. That
fact, along with the location of the property, had initially
grabbed Cal's interest. His team was already calling the property Pentagon II due to its shape and as a tribute to its larger
cousin just outside Washington, D.C.

Cal walked along the row of perfectly placed hedges that
flowed into the half moon back patio. In the center was a
round fountain pond. They still hadn't decided what to do
with the backyard other than to limit entry. Another item on
their ever-growing to-do list. Luckily Jonas would handle it.

Cal passed under the white columned portico, nodding to
a stern faced electrical contractor installing the wiring needed
to power the impressive array of technology that would soon
be delivered to the small headquarters. Jonas was inside
looking down at a set of blueprints laid out on the foldout
table they'd been using to eat on. He was talking to a short
Latino with a thick beard braided into twin strands below his
chin. The former delta operator everyone called Gaucho
looked up as Cal entered.

"Hey, boss. You gotta check out what Jonas is planning. Dude is gonna make this a fucking sweet joint."

Cal smiled, always amused by Gaucho's colorful personality. You'd never know by his near constant joking that the Mexican-American was deadly. He'd been one of Cal's first invitations, Gaucho joining the new organization along with eleven of his own operators.

"Let me go check my email and I'll be back down," said Cal.

"Boss, Snake Eyes was looking for you. I think he's in the War Room."

The War Room was a miniature version of the Situation Room in the White House and had been the first space they'd remodeled. Secured from the eyes of the constant stream of workers by a steel reinforced door, the War Room was the heart of their new venture.

Cal headed that way.

Once he'd entered his personal code and passed the retina scan, Cal pushed the door open. The space was about twenty by twenty feet; the walls lined with computers screens. A temporary conference table sat in the center of the room. That's where Daniel Briggs, aka Snake Eyes, the former Marine sniper, blond ponytail and all, sat analyzing a map. Daniel was one of Cal's closest friends and rarely left his boss's side. Part bodyguard and part advisor, the sniper oozed quiet confidence and a certain streak of luck that his friends liked to rib him about. Cal had never seen Daniel get so much as a scratch on the many operations they'd conducted together. Gaucho had once said that Daniel was blessed by God and that maybe everyone else should carry around a Bible like Snake Eyes.

Cal didn't know what to believe, but he did know that

Daniel was imbued with some kind of... Well, he just called it a gift.

"You were looking for me?" asked Cal, sidling up to see what Daniel was looking at. He instantly recognized it as a map of the surrounding area.

"Yeah. A call came in from Brandon. He wanted to see how things were going." Aside from Cal and his cousin, Daniel was on a very short list of people who could call the president by his first name.

"Do I need to call him back?" Cal wasn't a fan of people looking over his shoulder, even his friends.

"I think so. He probably just wants to see if he can lend a hand."

Cal rolled his eyes. He had enough to do without having to report in to the president. Maybe he hadn't made himself clear. He shook the orneriness away, constantly battling to control his short fuse.

"Okay."

Cal clicked the speaker button on the secure phone in the center of the conference table and pressed the only preset phone number there. It was labeled "Pres."

"Cal Stokes for the president, please."

"One moment, sir."

"Cal?"

"Good morning, your Holy and Mightiness. How may your humble servants be of even humbler service?"

The president chuckled. "You sure you don't want to join me in D.C.? I don't get enough ass-kissing up here."

"No way." The president knew that Washington, D.C. was one of Cal's least favorite places to visit, what with all the politicians and partisan bickering.

"Fair enough. How are things going?"

"Somehow we're ahead of schedule. It probably has to do with the way Jonas pays his people. I don't think the city of

Charlottesville had ever approved any renovation this quickly."

"He knows what he's doing."

"You've got that right."

"Good. Is there anything I can do to help?"

Cal bit back another smart remark. "I don't think so. Daniel, can you think of anything?"

Daniel shook his head.

"I think we're good," said Cal. "How's my cousin behaving?"

"You know Trav, steamrolling the assholes with a bulldozer."

It was Cal's turn to laugh. Although his cousin's disdain for politicians was more tempered than his own, Travis was still a no BS kinda guy. In the short time he'd been in the White House, the former SEAL had purged the non-performers and constructed what even the media considered a strong presidential team.

"Tell him I said hi."

"I will, and don't hesitate to call if you need anything. I mean that, Cal."

"I will. Thanks."

The call ended and Cal looked at Daniel. "Would you have thought two years ago that we could call the president of the United States whenever we wanted?"

Daniel shook his head. "No way."

NATIONAL INSTITUTES OF HEALTH (NIH) HEADQUARTERS

BETHESDA, MARYLAND - 9:51AM, APRIL 4TH

The muted walls of the corner office were plastered with black picture frames. Not the typical "I Love Me" items of a military veteran, but the remnants of death. A picture of a mass grave in Rwanda, bodies stacked like cords of wood outside a mill house. Numerous shots of victims of disease, wounds still seeping with pus, gashes oozing dark blood. Dead eyes everywhere.

New visitors to the space left either appalled or disgusted. There was no other way to respond. No one thought to ask its owner why he had such a grisly collection displayed so prominently.

There was a reason. Not unlike the gruesome images collected and hung precisely on his walls, the face of Army Colonel Gormon Cromwell spoke of pain and disease. The left side of his face sagged grotesquely, the after effects of some unknown bacteria he'd contracted while on assignment as a young captain in the jungles of central Africa. He'd been left for dead when he failed to check in with his team. It was only by sheer will and the aid of a nomadic huntsman that the Army Green Beret had stumbled back into camp a full week after disappearing.

His face swollen from infection, feet aching from immersion foot, and body racked with malaria, the local doctor had written him off. He said he'd seen the disease before, something the locals called 'the nodding disease.' The prognosis? Death. That was until Cromwell had pressed his always present pistol into the doctor's forehead and croaked, "You cure me or I'll kill you and all your people."

Whether it was the wild determination in the emaciated soldier's eyes, or the leveled rifle of the African huntsman who'd stayed on Gormon's side on promise of payment, the doctor relented, quickly calling in a team of Red Cross physicians.

He'd spent a month in that mosquito-infested clinic, finally attaining the needed stability to be transported back to Ramstein Air Base in Germany.

How had his superiors thanked him? They'd kicked him out of the green berets. They said he was in no shape to continue his career. More than one senior officer had suggested he medically retire, take his disability, and try to build a new life outside the military.

Cromwell would have none of it. He told them all. He forged a new career on his own. Instead of running from the diseases that had almost killed him, he embraced them. While recovering from his ailments, Cromwell pulled some strings and was accepted into Johns Hopkin's School of Public Health, earning a PhD in Global Disease Epidemiology and Control in half the time as prescribed.

Over the next fifteen years he'd become a legend, utilizing his former green beret skills along with his voracious appetite for unraveling the mysteries of infectious diseases to help contain outbreaks around the world.

Technically he was assigned to the Center for Disease Control (CDC) on loan to the National Institute of Health (NIH). Technically.

In reality, he now reported to a very small group of leaders who were nowhere in his chain of command. He'd become an anomaly, a soldier who wasn't afraid to make the tough calls within a broken bureaucracy. It had started off innocently enough. His real bosses at NIH would give him a small job and he'd take care of it. Small jobs led to bigger ones and pretty soon they never asked. When new bosses took the place of the old ones, they just assumed Cromwell was on his own, and that was fine with him.

It was one member of his unofficial hierarchy who he was on the phone with now.

"You know I wish I could help, but I don't see how."

"You know goddamn well what I'm asking. Don't be coy, Cromwell."

Col. Cromwell grinned. Of course he knew what the wily politician wanted. "Maybe if you tell me—"

"I could have you—"

"Now, I know how you must be feeling, but let's not say things today that we'll regret tomorrow."

Cromwell listened as his boss tried to get his temper under control.

"Fine. How much?"

"Ten million," Cromwell said without hesitating.

"You're kidding!"

"You know I only have a couple left."

"I don't have that kind of money!"

"I'm sure you could come up with it if you really thought about it. I could put in a call or two…"

"No. I'll handle it. When can you make delivery?"

"I can have a courier take it to you as soon I hang up."

"Good. And you'll take my word about the payment," asked the caller.

"Of course."

"I'll be waiting."

Cromwell looked out at his expansive view of the campus gardens and grinned. His retirement fund would almost double with this payment. Now, if he could only get his hands on Dr. Hunter Price and the rest of his stash.

CHARLOTTESVILLE, VIRGINIA

11:25AM, APRIL 4TH

Jonas had just finished explaining the impressive plans he'd developed for their new properties when the doorbell rang. Cal reached over and pressed the button on the video screen they'd had installed in each main room. Instantly the feed from the front door popped up.

There were three figures waiting, holding a variety of personal belongings. "Sorry, we already bought a case of Girl Scout cookies," said Cal into the microphone that patched to the outside speaker.

Two of the men on screen lifted their right hands and extended their middle fingers.

The four men assembled in the kitchen laughed as Gaucho went to let the three visitors in.

"You have correctly identified our secret password," said Cal in a bad British accent. "Our Mexican valet will be with you shortly."

"Fuck you, Cal," said Gaucho over his shoulder.

A moment later Gaucho reentered the kitchen with the

three men in tow. The first, a near seven foot muscle-bound former lineman with a flat top and bulging black arms, entered with an easy smile.

"I thought you boys would be out trying to round up some co-eds," said Marine Master Sergeant Willy Trent.

"Yeah," said Neil Patel as he walked in next, the dark complexioned Indian-American dressed impeccably as usual with a pair of lime green pants and a stylish form fitting sweater to match. His eyes smiled behind the stone colored Dolce & Gabbana glasses. The tech genius had an above 200 IQ score just like Jonas, and could hack into almost anything that was connected to an electrical outlet. He and Cal had first become friends at the University of Virginia, and it had been Cal who'd recommend his friend to his father for employment. Neil Patel made a lot of money for Stokes Security International, mostly through his constant tinkering and highly lucrative licensing deals. "You break in the Biltmore yet?"

The two men joined the others with handshakes and hugs. They'd been through a lot together. Other than Travis, these men were the only family Cal had left. He would gladly give his life for any one of them, and almost had on more than one occasion.

The last man stood back and watched the welcome. Shorter than the others and portly where the others were fit, Dr. Alvin Higgins, one of the top interrogators in the country, and probably the world, took it all in.

"I wasn't expecting you, Doc," said Cal, walking over to shake the old CIA employee's hand. While the Marine hated most shrinks, he loved Dr. Higgins. Behind his jovial facade lay a cold and calculating interrogator with the ability to extract information out of the most stubborn adversaries. His skills not only lay in the questioning, but in the apothecary-like crafting of potions that made criminals happy to tell the man in glasses, who liked the occasional pipe and talked like he could be from London, anything he asked.

"Nice to see you too, Calvin. Marjorie thought I might be of some use what with the change in SSI's role." Cal knew Higgins had made the last remark to see Cal's reaction, and despite trying, Cal couldn't help but wince.

"Does that mean you've decided to join our new fraternity?" asked Cal, the others now listening to the conversation.

"If you'll have me, I've already put in a call to an old friend at the medical school. Depending on what you need, I am prepared to join your fraternity, as you call it."

Cal couldn't help but smile. Having Higgins would seriously boost their capabilities. Not only was the good doctor indispensable with enemies in hand, he'd also been part of Travis's inner circle, the top of SSI, a highly valued part of the team.

"Are you kidding, Doc? We'd love to have you!"

There were cheers in the kitchen as they welcomed the last member of their team.

AFTER THE NEWCOMERS were shown to their temporary quarters (they were making do with multiple cots in each bedroom), the team gathered in the War Room to discuss their new mission. Cal took the lead.

"The president is giving us free rein. As long as we stay under the radar, we're golden," said Cal.

"What's our focus? Where do we start?" asked Trent.

"That's a good question, Top." (Top is what Marines affectionately called their Master Sergeants.) "One of the reasons Jonas is here—"

"You mean beside his billions?" interrupted Gaucho.

There was an awkward pause as everyone looked to Jonas, some of whom had just met him for the first time. The billionaire suddenly burst out laughing, and gave Gaucho a perfectly executed middle finger. "You got that right!"

The others joined in, realizing that maybe this new guy wasn't so bad.

"Now that Gaucho got the inappropriate comment out of the way, back to Top's question. Our mission hasn't changed much. We're still looking for bad guys and taking them down, but now we have a new tool. Jonas has a gift for predicting everything from stock swings to elections. I won't go into how he does it because, frankly, it's way over my head, but I think it'll help us track even better than we did before. The first step is to get him all the information he needs. Neil, that'll be your job. You two know each other so you can figure out how to coordinate the work flow. The rest of us will help pick and choose what's important and what's actionable."

"What do we do when we're not working?" asked Trent.

"Are you already itching for liberty, Top?" asked Gaucho.

"You know me, buddy, always lovin' libo. But seriously, until we get ramped up, I'm assuming we'll have some time to kill. Doc Higgins will be helping at the med school. What will the rest of us do?"

"I know a couple restaurants nearby that could use your culinary skills," said Neil, a smile tugging at the corner of his mouth.

Another middle finger and another round of chuckles.

"Other than helping out around here, you'll be free to come and go as you please. Same deal as SSI," said Cal. "If you want to take classes, I'm sure we can accommodate it, but the missions come first."

Heads nodded around the room. Cal knew how to take care of his men. He trusted them completely. They'd find ways to stay busy until their operational level spiked.

"What about training?" asked Gaucho. "Are we still allowed to use the SSI facilities?"

SSI kept a second headquarters just outside Charlottesville in Albemarle County, not ten minutes from where they stood. Camp Cavalier was almost an exact replica of Camp Spartan near Nashville, including just over 2,000 acres, live-fire ranges and training facilities.

"We'll have full use of both camps. We may not technically be part of the old company, but we're still part of the family," said Cal. "Any other questions?"

Dr. Higgins raised his hand. "What are we going to call this new outfit, Calvin?"

"It's funny you asked, Doc. That's the first thing we need everyone's help with."

GAINESVILLE, FLORIDA

12:20PM, APRIL 4TH

D r. Hunter Price breathed a sigh of relief as he shut the door to his dilapidated motel room, paint peeling in numerous round spots along the faded baby blue walls. He latched the bolt and rested his back against the wall, exhaling. For the last five hours, he'd gotten on and off public transportation, making sure he wasn't being followed. His body ached from the strain, brain thrumming.

This was one of three rooms he'd rented for a week, with cash, for his brief stay in Gainesville. He was in no rush. There was plenty of money left in his secret bank account, completely untraceable thanks to an old friend in the business. He still had to be careful, but his travel funds had the ability to sustain him for years. He was eternally grateful to a highly efficient financial planner who took very good care of his investments.

Hunter Price came from money. His entire family had gone to Yale, including his mother and his aunts. It's just what the Price family did.

It had all started with his grandfather, the stalwart Vincent Price, who'd immigrated to the United States from Poland shortly before the Second World War. Back then the family name was Koszt, which when asked about by the immigration official, was roughly translated to Price. From then on young Vincent embraced his new American name, enlisting as Private Price and being assigned to Gen. Patton's U.S. 2nd Armored Division and later in U.S. II Corps. He'd become one of Patton's favored translators due to his easy command of Polish, Russian and German.

Vincent Price left the Army during the post-war draw-down and used his military contacts to make a name in the business world. First opening a translation company that provided translators to the now divided Europe, he also found a new opportunity completely by accident.

On one of his trips overseas, Vincent purchased a glazed ornament for his new wife while traveling through Rome, a present for Christmas. Upon debarking, he happened to run into a wealthy business owner whom he'd met months before. The man asked Vincent about the package under his arm and Vincent showed him the beautiful ornament adorned with traditional Italian figurines.

The man's eyes went wide. Gushing over the craftsmanship, he offered Vincent an astronomical sum for the item that was purchased for mere pennies from a one-legged street vendor. Like any good businessman, Vincent sold the gift to the man and reinvested the proceeds in a gold bracelet for his wife.

The incident planted the seed for Vincent's new venture: importing. Through his friends both within the military and throughout Europe, Price's Imports soon became one of the leading importers in the Northeast. Within two years, Vincent had secured his family's future.

Years later, with his father's money, and at his urging,

Hunter's father, Vincent Jr., ran for political office as soon as he received his law degree from Yale. Aided by Vincent, Sr., Vincent Jr. rose quickly through the ranks of the New York State Legislature and then in the United States House of Representatives. If it weren't for his untimely death at the age of 40, Dr. Price had no doubt his father would still be in office.

Despite following in his family's footsteps when it came to college, Hunter wanted to go into the military like his grandfather. Vincent Sr. tried to dissuade his grandson from serving, pushing him to use his biology degree to become a doctor. Hunter finally relented, but only after accepting a Navy commission and a full scholarship to the Uniformed Services University of Health Sciences, a medical school dedicated to the training of military officers.

Due to his exceptional talent and high physical ability, Lt. Price's first duty station was with the SEALs in Dam Neck, VA. He'd been accepted by the elite warriors, and at one point considered putting in a request to go to Basic Underwater Demolition/SEAL Training (BUD/S). But a mission to Asia changed all that.

It was during that particularly scorching summer that three SEALs assigned to train Filipino Marines contracted an unknown illness. They'd medevaced the men with Lt. Price as their escort, landing in San Diego moments after Price had performed CPR on one of his patients, saving the man's life.

He'd seen firsthand the work of the dedicated scientists from the CDC who'd helped triage the men and luckily diagnosed and cured them.

The incident opened Price's eyes to a new world. While he loved his work with the SEALs, he knew his role would always be that of doctor, not operator. If he could somehow use his talents to eradicate deadly disease, he could help countless thousands if not millions.

With the blessing of his superiors, and a grudging nod from his grandfather, Hunter Price began his training with various branches of the CDC, with the intent of developing cures for some of the world's deadliest killers. He'd taken to the work with zeal; sometimes not going home for days so entranced was he by the power of tiny organisms that could wipe out an entire civilization if given the chance. Soon he had his own lab and a staff of three.

It was on an exploratory mission to South America where his life changed forever. It was there, with a reclusive tribe not known for its hospitality, that Price found a piece of the puzzle. So simple and yet able to help millions.

Dr. Price thought back to that moment as he lay down on the double bed that smelled like mildew, staring up at the water stained ceiling, the fan thumping softly. His life was so different now. His grandfather was dead. His own career was gone, and he was on the run. If only he could figure out a way...

He'd been over it time and time again. It was impossible to contact any of his former colleagues. He didn't know who he could trust. There was one person he knew he had to stay as far away from as possible: his old boss Col. Gormon Cromwell.

LOMBARDI CANCER CENTER

The halls bustled with activity, doctors and nurses shuffling from room to room. It was the smell in the place that bothered him, reminding him of his wife's death nearly a decade before. She'd been in a similar facility, dying right before his eyes. He'd made a silent promise never to step foot in another hospital, but that wasn't to be. He couldn't control everything, although he tried.

Senator Mac Thompson walked with a purpose, smiling at the hospital employees who glanced at the tall politician from Wyoming, giving him a wide berth. With auburn hair parted at the side and just now starting to gray, Mac Thompson looked like what a senator should be, strong and imposing. A former baseball star, Sen. Thompson clobbered opponents just as he'd hammered baseballs into the outfield.

He'd learned to temper his aggression, toning down his rhetoric and schmoozing with the best of Washington. Elected in a close battle with an incumbent Democrat, the

Republican swept into the senate full of exuberance and hope. While he had made his share of dents in the hide of the government beast, he'd also become accustomed to the life-style. Back when his wife was alive, they'd traveled constantly, eating at extravagant restaurants and staying in swanky hotels, all on someone else's dime.

Comfortable in his new role, the death of his wife had saddened him to the point of deep depression. Unlike so many other politicians in town, Mac Thompson had loved his wife as much as he had that first bright spring day in high school. They'd been together for close to thirty years when she passed. It had almost killed him.

The only thing that kept him from succumbing to his despair was his son. He was Thompson's sole heir, a miracle really. Countless doctors had said that Mindy Thompson would never conceive, but she did. It was a complicated birth, but twenty-five years before, Michael Thompson came into the world, screaming and healthy.

Michael represented all that was good in the senator's life. When fifteen year old Michael had lost his mother, he'd been the one to comfort his father, rarely leaving his side. They'd forged an iron bond since then, not a day going by that they didn't at least talk on the phone.

Those thoughts raged in his mind as Senator Mac Thompson stepped into the corner room, curtains thrown wide to let in the last rays of daylight. His son lay in bed staring at his cell phone, probably texting his girlfriend, a pretty little thing from South Carolina. Michael looked up when his father entered.

"Hey, Dad. I didn't think you were stopping by tonight."

Sen. Thompson leaned down and hugged his son, careful not to disturb the IV line affixed to his son's arm.

"Are you kidding? There's no place I'd rather be."

Michael rolled his eyes. "Whatever, Dad. You know you don't have to babysit me. Everything's taken care of."

Sen. Thompson patted his son on the shoulder, waiting until the lump in his throat passed so he could speak. *He looks so much like Mindy*. Weeks before, he'd received a call from the Georgetown University clinic. The physician's assistant had calmly told the senator that Michael, who was in the process of earning his law degree, had passed out at the gym. "He's doing fine, but we'd like to do some tests," she'd said.

The initial tests came back negative for anything obvious. Michael had insisted that he'd partied too hard over the weekend and probably hadn't hydrated properly. No novice to drinking, Sen. Thompson insisted that his son have a thorough examination. A day later the doctor came back with the verdict. It was small cell lung cancer.

"But he's so young. He doesn't even smoke!" Sen. Thompson had said to the doctor.

"Sometimes we don't know what causes it, Senator. I'll get a treatment plan to you right away."

The oncologist recommended chemotherapy. Treatment began and Thompson tried to be optimistic, but something in his gut told him it was bad. It was in the way the doctor glanced at him from time to time, as if expecting the powerful senator to rain down hail and brimstone should she fail to cure his son.

The first round of chemo had no effect, and the cancer spread quickly. Michael remained upbeat, but the weight started coming off and his energy levels waned. The senator's son was dying and there was nothing he could do. Almost.

"You want me to run out and get something from Five Guys? I'll bet you're sick of the hospital food by now," said the senator.

"I'm okay, Dad. It's not so bad." Michael yawned, his eyes drooping.

That was just like his son, always positive. Always looking on the bright side of a crappy situation.

"Why don't you take a little nap, son. I'll stick around until you wake up. I've got some emails to return."

Michael nodded, already half asleep. Two minutes later, he was snoring lightly. It was another detail he remembered from his wife's illness, a memory that banged inside his head. A light sleeper since they'd met, as soon as the cancer took hold, Mindy could doze off in the middle of a conversation. The same thing was happening to Michael.

Sen. Thompson held his son's hand for a moment, making sure he was out. Satisfied, he rose and closed the door, locking it carefully.

He walked over to the IV stand and extracted a syringe from his coat pocket, staring at it for a moment, grim determination making his heart beat faster. Saying a prayer to a God he wasn't sure he believed in, Sen. Thompson uncapped the needle and plunged it into the IV port.

Once finished, he returned the syringe to its original place and moved around the bed to resume his vigil. Taking his son's hand in his own, he whispered, "Everything's going to be okay, son. I promise."

CHARLOTTESVILLE, VIRGINIA

They'd sat into the night downing drinks and brainstorming ideas for the name of their new venture. There were the wacky ones like "Calvin's Heroes" and "Zimmer's Zoo." Through the laughing they were able to come up with some halfway decent ideas. It wasn't that anyone necessarily cared about the company name, but it was important to have some sort of identity that would help shape their cover.

In the end, no consensus was reached, the team opting to take what was left of the night to sleep on it.

Luckily, they'd cleaned up the mess they'd made the night before in the unfinished kitchen, because Cal's head was pounding. He almost tripped over a yellow level and tub of grout as he shuffled around the huge island, opening cupboards, trying to find a glass to get some water. Finally he found one, quickly filling the glass in the sink and downing its contents. One more and the cobwebs were starting to clear.

He was getting too old to be drinking with the boys. As if things couldn't get any worse, MSgt Trent stepped into the kitchen looking like he'd slept for a day. Refreshed and cheery.

"Good morning, boss. You ready for that run?"

Trent slipped a t-shirt over his head and walked to the fridge. Cal couldn't believe he'd promised to go for a run.

"Give me a couple minutes and I'll be ready," said Cal, trying to sound enthused but feeling the exact opposite. He'd have to remember not to attempt keeping up with Trent when they were drinking.

Trent looked over his shoulder and smiled. "Snake Eyes and Gaucho are out front waiting. Come out when you're ready."

Cal stifled a groan and went to his room to slip on his running shoes.

AN HOUR LATER, the runners returned, Cal finally feeling like himself. The first couple miles weren't any fun, but he'd managed to sweat out the fumes.

They stretched on the back porch, sipping from bottles of water provided by the ever helpful Daniel Briggs. The sniper didn't even look like he'd gone for a run, let alone a seven miler. Other than Trent, Daniel was one of the most physically fit individuals Cal had ever met. And that was saying something considering the company he kept.

"Beautiful campus," noted Gaucho, probably the only other one feeling the effects of the night before. Daniel didn't drink, so he didn't count.

"It's one of the reasons I fell in love with the place," said Cal. He remembered the first time he'd visited U.Va. Cal was touring colleges for the weekend, staying with a girl who'd been a year ahead of him in high school. They were just friends, but the perks of staying on the girl's floor had been a treat for the high school senior.

It was an early fall day in October. The leaves were just starting to change all over campus. Thomas Jefferson's university lived up to its reputation. Everyone was friendly and everyone wanted to be there. It came as a welcome change to Cal. He'd taken to the school instantly and hadn't seriously considered any others, although he'd applied to a handful.

"I heard you've gotta be pretty smart to get in a school like this. Who did the Colonel have to bribe to get you in?" asked Gaucho.

"Believe it or not, despite my foul mouth and poor attitude, I did pretty fucking well in high school," said Cal, remembering how proud his parents had been when he'd gotten his acceptance letter. His mother couldn't stop bragging for weeks.

"Do you really think they'll let us take classes?" asked Daniel.

"I told Jonas to look into it. If anyone can pull some strings it's him," said Cal.

The last few years had been a blur of activity for the former SSI men. If there wasn't an operation underway, there was another in planning stages. That didn't leave time for much other than family and work, and the four were all bachelors. Cal's father had always mandated that his employees spend time with their loved ones, a tradition that carried on through Travis and Cal. The Stokes men knew how to take care of their troops, and Cal meant to keep that up for as long as he had them.

"Well, if you're offering, I may look into getting my master's. Do they have a culinary department around here?" asked MSgt Trent, who'd managed to get a culinary degree from Johnston and Wales University. The others loved it when it was Top's turn to cook. He was always trying out some new recipe he'd concocted, and they were never disappointed.

Before Cal could answer, Jonas stepped outside carrying a thin green folder.

"You have a minute, Cal?" he asked.

"Yeah."

Cal rose from his stretching and moved to follow Jonas inside.

"Hey, Cal. Don't forget to ask Jonas about the culinary thing," reminded Trent, just as Cal closed the door.

"What did he want you to ask?" asked Jonas.

"Oh, nothing. He was just wondering if U.Va has a master's program for the culinary arts. I'm pretty sure they don't. Speaking of which, did you get any more information for the guys on taking classes?"

"I did. They'll have a couple different options depending on our schedule. I've talked to the president of the university, and she's more than happy to accommodate us."

"Just tell me how much it's gonna be and I'll take care of it." Cal had plenty of money from his ownership share of SSI. He could afford to pay.

"Don't worry about it. It's taken care of."

"You don't have to do that," said Cal.

"I want to. My treat. There is a catch, though."

"What's that?"

"Some of the deans, particularly the guy that runs the international affairs department, want to know if you guys would be interested in sharing some of your stories, give the kids some perspective."

"Really?" Cal didn't like telling war stories to strangers, but something about getting a chance to teach at his alma mater... Well, it was worth considering.

"It's not a requirement, but I'm sure the undergrads could learn a lot from you."

"Let me think about it. What did you want to talk to me about?"

"You're probably gonna think I'm crazy, but I ran across a string of interesting articles. Since we're still trying to figure out what our mission is, I thought you might want to take a look."

By that time they'd entered the War Room and Jonas was sitting in front of one of the many computers.

"What's the gist?"

"There have been reports of people miraculously being cured of cancer."

Cal resisted the urge to roll his eyes, wanting to give the newest member of the team a chance to take the lead.

"And this is important because...?"

"In every case I've tracked, the patient was terminal. Now, they weren't on their deathbed yet, but they had all been given diagnoses signing their death warrant. These people were going to die and then poof, the cancer was gone."

Cal cocked his head. "Are you telling me there's a pattern? How come nobody else is tracking this?"

"Hey, I'm good at what I do." Jonas smiled. "Now, I've plotted the ten cases I've found so far. Tell me if you notice a pattern."

Cal stared at the screen, analyzing the U.S. map clearly marked with ten red dots. Atlanta, Georgia. Columbus, Ohio. Williamsburg, Virginia. There wasn't a pattern that Cal could see.

"What am I missing here?" asked Cal.

"When I first analyzed it, taking the hospitals into account, nothing really jumped out as far as similarities. Different sizes. Different affiliations. Pretty random, actually. It wasn't until I went old school and just submitted all the cities into a generic web search that I got my answer. The first link Google showed me was to *U.S. News and World Report*'s annual college rankings. Every city has a public university listed as one of the top twenty colleges in the country."

"Wait. Are you saying you think the colleges are in on it?"

"Not really. I think, rather than doing it randomly, someone is using that list to administer the cure."

Cal shook his head. "I'm still not sure I'm tracking. Is this some conspiracy theory thing, because I don't have a clue what you want us to do about it."

"I haven't told you the best part yet. According to my analysis, and you know that I'm pretty fucking good at this kinda thing, I think the next cure will be at the number three public university in the country."

The hair on the back of Cal's stood. "And the number three school is..."

Jonas grinned. "The University of Virginia."

BOURBON STEAK RESTAURANT

GEORGETOWN - 11:34AM, APRIL 5TH

Senator Mac Thompson liked to take lunch early. The added bonus was missing the mad rush to get a table, and he hated being crowded. He loved Bourbon Steak, which was conveniently located on the ground floor of the Four Seasons Hotel in Georgetown, where he'd kept a room since Michael moved to the area. The head chef was a friend and liked to surprise the popular senator with delectable tastings that he generously hand-delivered to Thompson's room upstairs.

He'd called ahead, and they had his grilled hanger steak sitting in front of him not two minutes after he'd taken his seat. Situated in a nook farthest away from the popular lounge bar, Senator Thompson savored his first bite of perfectly medium rare steak, the hint of spicy peanut dressing adding to his enjoyment. There weren't many days that passed where he didn't eat some kind of red meat. He considered that fact as he gazed around the empty dining room, almost every decoration patterned in varying shades of brown, matching the steak on his plate.

There hadn't been a lot of red meat on the Thompson table when he was a child. His father had struggled to support his small family, often having to take up odd jobs out of town and send money home to his wife.

Truth be told, Mac Thompson knew his father was a simple man, but an honest one. Never in his life would he have considered a hand-out. His father believed in an honest day's work and helping your neighbor.

The fact that he'd somehow held on to the pastures handed down through three generations of Thompsons, despite his limited income, showed his father's resolve. There'd been times when it'd been so cold in the deep Wyoming winter that Mac and his younger brother had slept in their parents' bed, the tiny bedroom being the only room other than the kitchen with a wood-burning stove.

They'd been hard years, with young Mac learning early on the value of hard work and toil, but his parents had been loving. Mac excelled in sports and academics, receiving an athletic scholarship to play baseball at the University of Southern California. His mother and father had been so proud, scrimping and saving to make it to as many games as they could. His father had even been there to see Mac win the College World Series in 1973 against Arizona State.

He'd died of a heart attack later that year, leaving his wife, Miranda, with a pile of bills and a parcel of land the bank was eyeing for foreclosure.

Luckily, Miranda Thompson was something of a beauty, and she was quickly targeted by a local real estate developer named Darron Weber for courtship. The relationship started slow, mostly due to Mac's mother's concern for her two boys, the youngest, Jake, still a senior in high school. But Darron was a good man and a patient one. He'd settled the Thompson family's debts without the least bit of coercion.

So although he'd at first been angered by his mother's new relationship, Mac quickly saw how much Darron loved his mother, and she in return was learning to love him.

They waited until both Thompson boys graduated college to get married. Darron Weber had become a second father to Mac and Jake, teaching them about business and giving them their first taste of a better life. It was Darron who'd taken Mac out to dinner and bought the young man his first ribeye, bone in, of course. Senator Thompson remembered that the damn thing had been as large as his plate and he'd eaten it hungrily, savoring every bite. It was during that meal that Mac Thompson silently declared to the world that he would become somebody and would never lack for anything again.

He smiled as he looked back at all he'd accomplished. A loving family. Wealth. Power. His was a life to envy. Up until his wife's death, and now his son's illness, he'd thought the same. With his world unraveling, Sen. Thompson took the only path he knew, his path.

Just as he was finishing the last bite of cabbage slaw, his guest arrived, wearing a loose fitting grey suit, not well tailored. Certainly not to Sen. Thompson's standards.

"Have a seat, Colonel," he said, pointing to the chair across from him with his fork.

Col. Cromwell nodded and sat down without saying a word, his disfigured face a mask of intensity. That was one of the things Thompson hated about the man; he could never read his facial expressions. The senator figured that Cromwell knew that and used it to his advantage.

"I take it you received my payment?" asked Thompson.

"Yes, sir. Thank you."

"You're building quite a retirement for yourself, Colonel. I hope you're putting it somewhere safe."

Cromwell smiled, the gesture pulling his scarred skin grotesquely. "You know me, Senator, always watching my six."

Thompson nodded, not wanting to push the point farther. Cromwell had his uses, but the powerful senator preferred to keep the man at arm's length.

"Where are you in your search for the missing doctor?"

Cromwell took a sip of water, a tiny dribble escaping from the damaged corner of his mouth. He quickly wiped it away with his napkin. "We found him again, but he got away."

Sen. Thompson wanted to slam his fist onto the table, but took a steadying breath instead. "How is that possible?" he growled. "We've been looking for him for almost a year, for Christ's sake."

Cromwell shrugged, seemingly unconcerned. The movement made Thompson burn inside. They'd covered every other contingency, transferred old colleagues to far off laboratories, destroyed records. They'd even gone so far as to get rid of all traces of the thief's life. His identity had effectively vanished.

"He's a smart man, Senator, and I'm sure he is not without his own network of contacts."

"So find them and squeeze them for information, dammit."

"We're working on it. One of my staff thinks they may have found a banker who could be controlling the doctor's financials. If that turns out to be the case, we should be able to cut off the money supply."

At least that was something.

"Are you any closer to finding where he hid his files?"

"No, sir. He must have taken them with him. The good news is that we have a nationwide alert out with any lab that could provide him with the capability to replicate the strain. His options are limited and I'm sure his supply is dwindling."

"I know I don't have to tell you this, but we need him alive. Make sure your goon knows that."

Cromwell smiled again. "Don't worry about Mr. Vespers, Senator. He's very good at his job."

MIRAMAR BEACH, FLORIDA

1:45PM, APRIL 5TH

He gazed out over the emerald green water, breathing in the cool salt air from his seat on the white sand. There was a young family with a giggling toddler playing in the surf, jumping the small waves that lapped onto shore.

Dr. Hunter Price loved the beach. The first time he'd visited Florida was with his grandfather. They'd come through after a business trip to New Orleans. Back in those days his grandfather let him tag along, sharing bits of business and lessons of manhood along the way. They always drove even though the trip from the Northeast was long.

After his grandfather's death, he'd continued his trips to the Florida Panhandle. So many memories. Before, it was his way to escape the stresses of his job and remember his grandfather. Now it was brief respite on his way to another town. Part of him enjoyed the thrill of the vagabond lifestyle. Another wanted to settle down, maybe find a wife and have some kids.

But that wasn't possible. He was on the run. He no longer

had an identity. Anything of importance had been stripped from him. He was like a ghost, haunting his former employer, living a half life in the shadows.

Price took a pull from his bottle of beer, wishing he could stay on the beach forever. It was like it was calling him saying, "Stay and forget everything else."

He couldn't. As stupid as it sounded, he felt like he had an obligation to keep going, to show the world what was possible. Finishing the last swig of beer, he reluctantly pushed himself up and took a long look at the ocean. It was time to get back to work.

HE'D FOUND a cheap room just off the main strip. It was actually a subdivided trailer owned by a middle-aged divorcee by the name of Janice who was happy to take his cash in exchange for a week's rental. He wouldn't be in town that long, but most places were less likely to ask questions if you paid for a full week in advance.

Price ducked under the sagging aluminum awning, dodging the drops of brown rust water dripping into a murky puddle. Entering his tiny room, he threw his backpack on the bed and flopped down next to it. The cheap bed sagged under his weight, creaking with the effort as he closed his eyes. A moment later, the cell phone in his pocket buzzed. Price tensed at the sound. There was only one person who knew how to reach him. He pulled it out carefully, praying for a wrong number. It wasn't.

He answered the call.

———

WILMINGTON, DELAWARE

It had been a very bad morning for Brad Turnberry. First, he woke up with a raging hangover, memories of the celebratory drinks the night before a fading wisp. Luckily, his wife was out of town on a girl's trip or she would have given him the 'I told you so' eyes.

Just as he dragged himself out of the bathroom for the fourth time, his phone rang shrilly, making his gut clutch. It was his boss. He'd been at the party with Brad the night before. He sounded almost as bad as Brad felt.

"Hey, I need you to meet me at the office. We've got some Fed assholes coming in to look at a couple of your clients."

The mention of the Feds shouldn't have bothered Brad, especially with the increased scrutiny after the latest economic slide, but this time he had reason to worry. Normally a by-the-book banker and financial planner, he had one client that was getting harder and harder to hide.

"Okay. I can be at the bank in fifteen minutes."

The two Feds were waiting in his office when he arrived.

"I'm sorry to keep you waiting gentlemen. I'm Brad." He moved to shake the two men's hands, pausing when he got a look at the shorter man's face. There was something wrong with the left side of it. *Stroke?* The man didn't offer his hand and Brad took the hint, taking his position behind his desk.

"I'm sure your boss let you know why we're here, Mr. Turnberry."

"Yeah. He said something about you wanting to take a look at some of my accounts."

The man with the warped face nodded.

"We have an ongoing investigation concerning an escaped fugitive."

Sweat broke out on Brad's back despite the cool temperature in the room. The hangover wasn't helping.

"And you think one of my clients is involved?"

"What can you tell us about Frank Rounders, Mr. Turnberry?"

"I...I'll have to look that up." He glanced to the man in black sunglasses, who had yet to say a word. "I'm sorry. I don't mean to be rude, but I forgot to ask your names and who you're with."

"My name is Cromwell and this is my associate Mr. Vespers. We're with the Securities and Exchange Commission. Would you like to see our identification?" The question came out as more of a dare than a friendly offering.

Brad shook his head. "I don't think that'll be necessary. Now, let me see what I can find about Mr. Roundup, did you say?"

"Rounders. Frank Rounders. But you may know him better as Dr. Hunter Price."

Brad tried not to let the shock show, but he felt himself pause, trying to avert his gaze toward his computer screen. Moisture tickled his upper lip, seeping out of the pores on his forehead.

"Doesn't ring a bell," he said a bit too hastily.

While he did his best to look like he was clicking through files, his head spun, trying to come up with a plan. Cromwell watched. Vespers stood and walked to first one, then the second window facing the interior of the bank, closing the blinds, then locking the door.

Brad felt whatever contents were left in his stomach churn. He somehow held back the acidic bile in the back of his throat. His mind began panicking as he noticed Mr. Vespers out of his peripheral vision moving around the desk.

"I think I've got...yeah, here's the account," Brad blurted, hoping that would make the imposing Vespers retake his seat.

"I want you to freeze all accounts owned by Hunter Price," said Cromwell.

"You mean Rounders?" asked Brad.

Cromwell nodded to Vespers, who pulled out a silenced pistol and pointed it straight at Brad's shocked face.

"How about we stop playing around, Mr. Turnberry. We know about your relationship with Dr. Price. High school friends. Both went to Yale. Ran cross country together. Should I go on?"

Brad shook his head, all blood drained from his face.

Cromwell continued. "We also know that your wife is currently spending a relaxing long weekend in Cabo San Lucas with her three friends Michelle, Jen and Lilly. Would you like to know what they had for breakfast?"

Brad shook his head again, trying his best to stop shaking. The tip of the suppressor now rested against his temple, Vespers's face placid.

"Here's what I want you to do. First, wire the contents of Price's accounts to this account," Cromwell reached over the desk and set an index card in front of Brad.

For some reason Brad didn't scream or call out for help. Later he would realize that the threat of physical violence had completely paralyzed him. Instead of yelling he tried to focus on his task, hoping that the two men would just leave after he finished. He hoped Hunter would understand.

"Okay. It's done," he announced.

Cromwell nodded and did something with his phone, probably confirming the transfer.

"Very good, Mr. Turnberry. Now, I want you to pick up your cell phone and call Dr. Price."

That was when Brad's bladder failed him, warm urine wetting his thigh then running down his leg into his shoes. "But, I—"

"Let's not do this again, Mr. Turnberry. We know you've been in periodic contact with your old friend. I give you my word that as soon as I finish my conversation with Dr. Price, we'll leave your office and never come back."

It didn't take long for Brad to decide. With shaky hands he picked up his cell phone and dialed a number from memory. Hunter had told him to only use it in case of an emergency.

The call rang twice and Hunter picked up. Brad didn't say a thing, handing the phone to Mr. Vespers, who handed it to his boss.

"Hello, Dr. Price."

MIRAMAR BEACH, FLORIDA

3:42PM, APRIL 5TH

Dr. Price gripped the phone, panic spreading into his chest, its cold fingers reaching for his pounding heart. The raspy sound of his old boss's voice made him want to scream. The man was a monster, no different than Hitler or Stalin. While at first Price had sympathized with Cromwell's mission, he'd soon come to see the truth of it. Cromwell didn't give a damn about anyone, except perhaps his trusted employee Malik Vespers. Their relationship was the only touch of emotion left in Cromwell.

"What did you do with Brad?" asked Price, fearing the worst.

"Hello to you too, Dr. Price. I'm hurt that you haven't called."

Price could picture his enemy's face, cruel and unyielding. Lethargic on one side, always intense on the other. It was a vision he saw in his nightmares, Cromwell on black wings swooping down like a banshee as he ran for cover.

"Tell me what you did with Brad."

"He's sitting across from me. Of course, Mr. Vespers has a gun pressed to his head, but other than that and a little piss in his pants, Mr. Turnberry is fine."

"What do you want?"

"I want you to come in. We've got work to do."

"I don't work for you anymore, remember? Besides, didn't you wipe out any trace of my existence?"

Cromwell chuckled. "What did you expect? You left in the middle of the night and took my property with you."

"I know what you were planning. There isn't a chance in hell that I'll help."

"Even if that means we have to shoot poor Mr. Turnberry?"

Price heard a muffled moan in the background. He winced, easily imagining what Cromwell would do with his friend. He'd seen it before, including the body of the man they'd said was him, the one that had washed up on the shores of the Potomac.

"I'm waiting, Dr. Price."

"What assurance would I have?"

"Call it my word as an officer and a gentleman."

Price would've laughed out loud were the circumstances different. Cromwell had endlessly besmirched the honor of the Army uniform he sometimes wore, and to call himself a gentleman was preposterous. It was like calling Charles Manson a boy scout.

"That's not good enough."

"I don't think you're really in a position to argue, doctor. We know where you are and we have your money."

"You fucking—"

"Now, now, doctor. Why don't you just turn yourself in and we'll get back to work."

Price seethed. He was trapped. Sure he had more money hidden away, but he'd been careful. Brad controlled close to ninety percent of his accounts under various aliases including, Frank Rounders.

I should have put a bullet in Cromwell's head when I had the chance.

Instead of continuing the conversation, Price said a silent prayer for Brad and ended the call. It only took him a moment to gather his possessions and step outside, dropping the cell phone on the gravel pavement and stomping it into the ground.

His decision made, Dr. Price headed for the nearest bus station and his next destination. He had a mission to complete.

―――――

WILMINGTON, DELAWARE

Cromwell handed the cell phone back to Brad and nodded to Malik Vespers, who replaced the pistol in its holster. Brad hadn't taken the conversation well, twice vomiting into his stainless steel trashcan.

"Thank you again for your assistance, Mr. Turnberry. We'll be on our way."

The two men in suits walked to the door, Vespers leading. Just before he exited, Cromwell turned back to Brad, whose head was resting on his soiled desk.

"I suggest you find some new friends, Mr. Turnberry. As far as you're concerned, Hunter Price no longer exists."

―――――

AFTER REGAINING a measure of his composure, and changing into a set of seldom used workout gear he kept in his office, Brad Turnberry told his boss that he'd taken care of the situation with the Feds, but was going to take an early lunch.

"Can I join you? My treat. I'm finally getting my appetite back."

Brad did his best to look his friend in the eye and smile. "Mind if I take a rain check? I've gotta run home and clean up the place before Viv gets back," said Brad.

His boss chuckled and waved goodbye as Brad rushed to leave, feeling another vomit attack coming.

By the time he pulled into his garage, his stomach and heartbeat had settled. While the events of the morning hadn't been pleasant, at least the drama with Hunter was over. Sure they were friends, but he'd been in one helluva spot. Brad felt lucky that the two Feds hadn't taken his securities license, or worse, thrown him in federal prison. He knew what could happen to bankers who knowingly dealt with fugitives, and it was never pretty. There'd been a handful of acquaintances who'd shared that fate in the wake of the Wall Street debacle not a decade earlier.

No, it was better that it was over. He'd move on and Hunter would have to take care of himself. Hell, the guy came from money. He had to have more somewhere. Sure, the millions Brad had transferred to the account that Cromwell guy gave him would hurt, but Hunter was a smart guy, a doctor no less.

That's what Brad told himself as he entered his house, desperately needing a second shower, his body sticky with sweat and piss. He was so consumed with his thoughts that he didn't notice the shadow descend like a wraith, a strong arm wrapping around Brad's neck, muscles clamping down on his windpipe.

Malik Vespers didn't let go, not through the thrashing or the release of Brad's bowels. One minute, then two. Once he was sure Brad was dead, Vespers dragged the body to the tan microsuede couch, propping Brad up in the corner. A moment later he was back with a half-smoked cigar, its end still burning, and two liquor bottles, one a bottle of Bacardi 151 and the other a bottle of Everclear grain alcohol.

Vespers placed the cigar in Brad's left hand and poured the equivalent of a couple shots down the cadaver's throat. Then, after making sure the cigar was still lit and had already burned a portion of skin on Brad's hand, Vespers poured a liberal amount of both bottles over the body and onto the couch and floor. With a lighter, he lit the flammable liquids and stepped back as the blue flames took, quickly engulfing Brad and the couch.

Normally Vespers would have worried about the trace evidence, but an advance team had already disabled the smoke detectors in the home, simply taking out the batteries. It was common for lazy homeowners to pull out a battery from a beeping alarm and forget to replace it. By the time the fire department arrived, Brad and his living room would be charred to a crisp.

Happy with his handiwork, Malik Vespers exited through the back door, walked around the house, and entered the waiting black tinted SUV.

"Done?" asked Col. Cromwell from the back seat.

Vespers nodded, once again happy that he could please his master.

CHARLOTTESVILLE, VIRGINIA

7:20PM, APRIL 5TH

The War Room hummed with activity. Cal's men had separated into groups, happy to be working on something, even if it did sound crazy. Luckily, they'd installed upgraded central air ducts in the workspace or else it might've been stifling.

Cal and Daniel were sitting beside Jonas and Neil, who'd been swapping tech lingo for the past four hours, trying to come up with some way to find out who or what administered the supposed cancer cure. One of the first places they'd looked was the suppliers for the IV liquids and medications, but that turned out to be a dead end. Only a handful of the hospitals used the same suppliers and the likelihood of a major drug corporation randomly, yet not so randomly, dispersing the drugs was unlikely.

Neil's software was in the process of filtering through thousands of hours of video feed, trying to get a hit. Nothing yet.

"Come on, guys, there has to be some way we can figure out who is doing this," said Cal, feeling worthless as he looked on.

"I think it's just gonna take time," said Neil.

"For all we know they've come and gone, already on their way out of Charlottesville," said Cal.

Jonas shook his head. "Unlikely. According to the time-lines I've built, I think we have a day or two until our window. Neil's right. Just give it some time."

Without further guidance from the president, and because they were still getting their own assets in place, there wasn't much Cal could do. He looked at Daniel who, as usual, sat placidly, digesting everything around him.

"You have any ideas?"

Daniel took a moment before answering. "Let's do it the old-fashioned way."

"And what's that?" asked Cal.

"Let's set up surveillance in the most likely spots around the hospital and see what happens."

"But we don't even know who we're looking for."

Daniel shrugged. "We might get lucky."

Cal didn't like it. They could have men on the ground for days without anything to show. The more he thought about it, the more he wished he hadn't let Jonas convince him to undertake the investigation. Before he could voice his thoughts, MSgt Trent walked over with Gaucho.

"I'll volunteer for the first watch," said Trent.

"Me too, boss," said Gaucho.

Cal looked up at his men, then around the room at the others who'd stopped what they were working on to see what their leader would say. The Marine shook his head, but smiled.

"Okay. Gaucho, you and your boys take the lead on this one. Plug us in wherever you need."

"You got it."

Gaucho and Trent moved to rejoin the rest of the troops, who were already grouping their chairs into the middle of the room. Cal couldn't believe how excited they were about a boring surveillance mission until he realized that these men, these warriors, were accustomed to action. They'd lived and breathed combat and covert operations for years. Now they were stuck in some fixer-upper, waiting for him to come up with something to do.

Daniel must have read his mind because he nodded to Cal with that all-knowing grin.

Cal laughed and pointed at his friend. "Keep it up, Snake Eyes. You won't be smiling ten hours into the stakeout."

————

EN ROUTE TO REAGAN NATIONAL - 8:05PM, APRIL 5TH

Col. Cromwell and Malik Vespers were the only passengers on the Gulfstream V. The crew had been asked to stay out of the main cabin for the duration of the flight. There was work to do, and despite the crew's security clearance, Col. Cromwell did not want to be overheard.

To ensure complete privacy, Malik Vespers stood next to the front hatch leading to the cockpit where the flight staff was. Cromwell sat at the rear of the aircraft staring into the wall mounted screen, earbuds in place. He watched the shadowy figures of the other callers, wondering why the rest of the men chose to be cloaked in supposed secrecy even though each member of the elite group knew the others. They'd been arguing for the better part of an hour; round and round the powerful figures went trying to insert their opinions.

"Gentlemen," said Cromwell. The arguing continued. "Gentlemen." More forcefully.

It was Senator Mac Thompson who finally noticed Cromwell's voice. A bell sounded, it's ringing stopping the heated back and forth.

"Ladies and gentlemen, I think Colonel Cromwell has something to say," announced Sen. Thompson.

"I think Colonel Cromwell has said quite enough for today, Mac," said a shadow-cloaked figure who was obviously massively overweight. Cromwell knew the man and hated him. The CEO of Hampstead Healthcare had never hidden his contempt for the soldier either, trying more than once over the past years to have Cromwell replaced by someone of his own choosing. Not that it bothered Cromwell. He knew he was one of a kind, a man who would do what others wouldn't. What was still surprising to Cromwell was that Waldo Erickson, the CEO in question, couldn't see how similar he was to the military veteran. Ruthless.

"Let's see what he has to say. Colonel?" said Sen. Thompson.

"Thank you, Senator. As I explained at the beginning of our call, I believe the situation is contained. If we—"

"Contained?" blasted Erickson, his ample chin visibly jiggling despite the darkness doing its best to cover him. "You've failed, Cromwell. Doctor Price should be dead by now and his files recovered. Please explain to me once again why we should listen to any more of your bullshit excuses."

Cromwell was used to Erickson's bellowing. He didn't take the bait. "As I've told you before, we believe the best course of action is to take Doctor Price back under our control and allow him to assist us in our ongoing efforts."

"Because that worked so well before?" snarled Erickson.

"I admit that we missed the warning signs prior to Price's

departure, but I did offer my resignation at the time, and if I remember correctly, my retention was almost unanimous."

Erickson chuckled, the only dissenting vote at the time. "If you couldn't control him a year ago, what makes you think you can do it now?"

Cromwell smiled. "I'll soon have all the incentive he'll need."

CHARLOTTESVILLE, VIRGINIA

6:27AM, APRIL 6TH

Cal yawned between sips of coffee. It had been long night and another early wake-up. He'd relieved a grinning MSgt Trent, who seemed no worse off after his six hour shift in the hospital waiting room. It had been less than thirty minutes and already Cal was regretting his decision to agree to the stakeout.

Daniel sat a row away, reading a magazine, seemingly entranced by whatever lay within its pages. Cal knew better. The sniper was always vigilant. Daniel saw everything.

Cal scanned the patients, family and staff who filtered in and out of the muted waiting room outside the entrance of one of the five patient care units Jonas picked as likely ingress routes.

Gradually, Cal found his gaze pulled back to the nurse manning the secure door, turning away visitors with the efficiency of a drill instructor. Her countenance was always kind, but her body language assured no argument. She knew her job well.

It made Cal think.

How would I get in there?

The post-9/11 world included all sorts of heightened security, oftentimes making criminal acts less likely, but sometimes making it easier, as corporations and even government agencies relied too heavily on technology. Although Cal loved technology that could enhance his operational efforts, he'd never once considered it a valid alternative to a warrior with a weapon in his hand, or even a veteran nurse manning a door.

Human nature allowed for errors. That fact had been repeated countless times over the centuries. Sleeping sentries. Sloppy police work. Subpar attention to detail.

Human error. Human error. For some reason the words replayed over and over in Cal's head. He couldn't shake it. Like a resilient pit bull, the thought clung to his subconscious with stubborn urgency.

Then the original question pierced through the haze. *How would I get in there?*

The answer came a moment later. Cal sat up a little straighter, suddenly wide awake.

I'd have to be a doctor.

Cal pulled out his phone and texted Neil. *Focus your video scans on anyone dressed as a doctor.*

Neil replied a moment later with a curt, *Done.* At least the tidbit might narrow down the search. Cal settled in once again, this time taking care to look at every man and woman dressed in scrubs or a lab coat.

———

DR. PRICE DIDN'T like cutting corners, but this time would have to be the exception. Unable to get access to the bulk of his remaining funds, he'd decided to speed up his timeline. Where usually he would've taken a day or two to case a new hospital, this go-around he'd have to administer the dosage on the first day. It was either that or he'd have to find a park to sleep in.

Walking out of the lobby of the Red Roof Inn, a cup of stale coffee in his right hand, a soggy danish in his left, Hunter Price made his way through the throng of young adults moving in the opposite direction. He looked like one of them. Young. In shape. Slightly harried.

Walking at a brisk pace, he crossed the familiar intersection and followed old memories to his destination. He'd dated a girl who'd been an intern there before. The occasional weekend romp hadn't lasted though, his hectic work schedule always a strain. She'd married some lawyer in Fairfax, or was it Alexandria?

It didn't matter. Never one with enough time to have a family, or at least that's what he'd told himself as he traveled from hotspot to hotspot, Hunter Price wondered what it would be like to settle down, and whether he'd live long enough to have the chance.

Seeing his final stop up ahead, Dr. Price picked up his pace, grasping one of the straps on his backpack a little tighter. His nerves were shot, and he tried to glance around casually, knowing that he must look like a mess. But that was okay. Part of him knew that he'd fit right in. There was no shortage of stressed med-students in and around the hospital. In fact, two stepped up beside him as he got closer to the Emergency Room door. They looked worse than he did, faces sagging, dark bags under their eyes, both carrying the biggest cup of Starbuck's coffee money could buy.

Price paused as if he'd stepped on something, letting the two students go ahead. He fell in behind them, mimicking their bedraggled shuffle.

———

CAL WATCHED as a group of overworked med students entered, each showing their ID badges to the nurse working the door. He could tell that she recognized most of them, nodding and smiling politely. Cal wondered whether she felt any love for her future superiors at all.

Three groups in, one of the soon-to-be-doctors actually got stopped by the gatekeeper. Cal couldn't hear what she was saying, but the guy looked embarrassed, patting his pockets and finally whipping his backpack around to see if he'd somehow stowed the key there.

A moment later, the relieved looking student pulled out his ID and was buzzed through by the nurse as she cast a wary eye as he went.

Five minutes later, Cal's phone buzzed and he took it out of his pocket, examining the text from Neil. *Keep an eye out for this guy. Fits the timeline.*

There was a set of three grainy photos. Cal had found the best way to look at pictures that had less than adequate resolution was to almost look through them, let them blur so you got more of feel for the shape of the faces rather than any specific details. He did this with the images Neil had sent and alarm bells instantly went off in his head. He'd seen that face before, Cal was sure of it.

Where?

Cal closed his eyes, tilting his head back as he processed the endless stream of people coming through the waiting area. Then it hit him. The guy who couldn't find his ID.

Coughing in his hand to get Daniel's attention, he motioned to the corner table that held a collection of old magazines. Daniel nodded and followed him over.

Cal handed his phone to the sniper who, unsurprisingly said a second later, "The guy with the backpack who couldn't find his badge."

Nodding, Cal ran through their options. They were

already spread thin, their small teams watching over five loca-tions. He was taking a chance if he called everyone in, espe-cially if it was just a coincidence. Sixteen guys descending on an unarmed civilian in broad daylight wasn't the best of ideas.

"You stay here. If the guy comes out, follow him and let me know where you're headed. I'll go to the rear exit we picked and tell the guys that just got off watch to head this way. Should give us good coverage."

Daniel nodded and took his seat. He knew what to do.

Working from memory, Cal made his way out of the building and toward the rear exit that did not allow reentry. It was the most likely escape route, and there he would wait.

————

DR. PRICE'S heart felt like a heavy metal drummer was pounding away at it after snorting a few lines of coke. How could he have been so stupid? He'd swiped the ID badge the night before from a med student at The Biltmore Grill who'd had more than his share of whiskey and had roughly the same features as Price. But to forget to put it on? He was beyond blessed that the nurse at the door hadn't looked closer at the picture or else he would've had a helluva situation to deal with.

Ten minutes later, his drug administered, Dr. Price made his way through the winding corridors to the back exit, shed-ding his layers of scrubs along the way. He exhaled in relief as he pushed through the door and stepped outside.

CHARLOTTESVILLE, VIRGINIA

7:39AM, APRIL 6TH

Cal took a seat on one of the many pre-Civil War era stone walls lining greenways across campus. The spot gave him a good vantage point of two rear hospital exits. Behind one sat two janitors who'd propped the one-way door open with a brick. They sat chatting and smoking lazily, in no rush to get anywhere.

His senses tingling, Cal watched the steady stream of people walking by. Students. The odd professor. A tourist or three. A perfect place to get lost in a crowd.

Cal had his Springfield XD .45 tucked in his waistband, ready for use. He doubted he'd have any need for it, but that, along with the double edged knife tucked in a wrist holster on his left arm, kept him prepared at all times.

There shouldn't be any need for force. Hell, Cal and his band of warriors still didn't have a clue what they were dealing with, just a hunch from Jonas.

Without anything left to do but wait, Cal did just that.

NOW DONNING a faded blue Virginia cap he'd purchased with the last cash in his pocket, Price scanned the area from under the bill. Comfortable in his pair of running pants and a well-worn white T-shirt, he took off down the sidewalk, fading into the stream of travelers.

CAL WATCHED the man in the blue ball cap and white T-shirt exit the building. *That's the same guy.*

He texted the rest of his team and set out to follow the suspect, still not sure of what he'd do or say when he caught up to the guy.

DR. PRICE'S mind worked to process the busy street, wary of any onlookers. He didn't see anything suspicious, but that didn't mean no one was watching. His enemies were cunning and skilled.

A familiar prickle ran up his neck, tickling his scalp. Not one to doubt his senses, Price stepped to the curb, deciding to cross the street, glancing both ways as if looking for a break in the traffic, when in fact he was looking for a tail. Nothing. Everyone looked the same.

But still, he felt that nagging urge to run. He resisted, instead waving his thanks to the two drivers who stopped to allow him to cross Jefferson Park Avenue, heading toward the heart of the campus, or as he'd just remembered U.Va students called it, Grounds.

He picked up his pace as he hit the opposing sidewalk, slipping through the throng of kids heading to class.

———

CAL LET his target cross first, taking his time to do the same. He knew the campus well and his team was closing in. It was only a matter of time before they cornered the man.

A half a block later, Cal crossed Jefferson Park Avenue and picked up the pace.

———

STILL PART of the line of students, Price walked into the back of New Cabell Hall, deciding to make a few passes up and down the stairwells and classroom hallways. The sensation of being watched hadn't subsided and he resisted the urge to bolt. Instead, he plastered a bored look on his face and made his way up the stairs.

———

CAL TEXTED the rest of his team and told them to cover the New Cabell Hall exit. He reiterated that they not make a scene. That was the last thing they needed. Colleges were even more frightened at the thought of having weapons on campus. Every one of Cal's men was armed. All it would take was a tiny altercation for the authorities to be called.

His team knew the better way was to maintain surveillance and hopefully confront the suspect away from Grounds.

Satisfied that his team was in place, Cal slipped into the building, barely catching a glimpse of a blue hat up ahead.

———

THE WARNING BELLS in Price's brain blared like a klaxon.

He'd seen the face of a man who he thought he recognized from earlier. Young. Fit.

Adrenaline hiked his blood pressure, his breathing increased. A trickle of sweat ran down his back as he ducked into an empty classroom on the third floor. Hustling to the back of the space, he sat in a chair and pulled his backpack off, laying it on the desk in front of him. His hand now held his loaded Glock inside the zipper. He didn't want to use it, but he would if needed.

———

CAL SAW the guy duck into a classroom. Instead of following, he made a discreet pass to see if there was a class in session. Nope. Empty.

He quickly texted the room number to his team. They'd be there in a moment. Taking a deep breath, Cal opened the door and stepped inside.

———

PRICE'S BODY tensed as the same face he'd seen outside walked into the classroom. Without hesitation he stood, slipping his weapon out of the backpack and aimed at the man.

"Put your hands—"

Before he could finish, the good-looking guy whipped out his own pistol.

"Don't do anything stupid, buddy."

———

THE GUY'S pull was quick, practiced. It had taken Cal by surprise. He stared down his sights, wondering what the guy

was thinking. For a moment they just stood there, no sound except for the muffled footsteps from the hallway.

"I already told Cromwell I'm not coming in," said the man.

"I don't know any Cromwell, dude. Now why don't you lower your weapon and I'll do the same."

His opponent cocked his head, eyes taking him in.

"You're full of shit," said the guy.

Cal shrugged. "Sometimes. I'm a Marine. I can't help it."

———

THE STRANGER'S demeanor confused Price. He didn't look like one of Cromwell's goons. He sure as hell didn't act like one either.

"How do I know you don't work for Cromwell?" asked Price.

The supposed Marine exhaled and put one hand in a' lowering his weapon. He surprised Price farther by bend down and setting the pistol on the ground.

"Happy now?"

———

DESPITE STILL HAVING a loaded weapon aime was calm. The guy didn't look like he was ne never once dropped his gaze and had even r from the trigger when Cal had placed ground.

"Why are you following me?" the curious.

Cal scratched his head. "That's '

"Who do you work for?"

"That's an even longer story

The man coughed out a sarcastic laugh. "Tell me why I shouldn't tie you up and leave you."

Cal was tired of the back and forth. "Look. We know about the cancer thing."

The guy's eyes widened, his finger once again jumping to the trigger. "How did you—"

"Like I said, it's a long story. Listen, I've got a place right around the corner. How about we head over there and talk this out?"

"No thanks. I think I'll go in the other direction."

"I'm sorry you feel that way."

CHARLOTTESVILLE, VIRGINIA

9:04AM, APRIL 6TH

Price's finger tightened on the trigger. He could feel the pressure keenly, knew how much it took to make the weapon fire. Countless rounds downrange. He expected his adversary to go for his weapon. What happened instead surprised him even more.

Before he had a chance to respond to the cocky guy standing there with an annoyed look on his face, three more men rushed into the room, weapons trained on him. Price did a quick appraisal of the new arrivals.

A guy roughly the size of the first, but this one with his blond hair tied back in a pony tail. Eyes steady like a snake about to strike. The second, a huge black guy who would've had to duck to get inside the door had he been standing straight up. He looked like an NFL lineman. The third a short Hispanic with a funny looking beard weaved in twin braids hanging off of his chin. He could tell they all meant business. No hesitation. All pro.

"Put the gun down, sir," said the black giant.

Price knew he was cornered. All he could do was nod and lower his weapon.

———

CAL WAS RELIEVED when the guy finally put his weapon on the ground. Daniel moved to secure the firearm along with the man's backpack. Gaucho frisked the man, giving Cal a curt nod when finished.

"I think we can put those away now, guys," said Cal. His friends re-stashed their weapons, but still kept a wary eye on their target. "Let's head back to the house and chat. Can you make the trip without making a run for it? He may look like a slow beast, but Master Sergeant Trent can outrun the rest of us in a foot race."

The man nodded, his shoulders sagging.

After retrieving his own weapon, Cal walked up with his hand extended. "Cal Stokes, Mister...?"

"Price. Doctor Hunter Price."

———

THE FOUR MEN escorted Dr. Price up to the Lawn side exit facing Thomas Jefferson's famous Rotunda at the far end. Workers were busy doing something to its once white dome. Lush moss green grass blanketed the interior of the Lawn, students taking advantage of the early sun to lay back and soak in its rays. Some were throwing Frisbees or footballs.

Price wasn't sure, but he felt more eyes on the periphery, probably with this Cal Stokes and his men. It was obvious that the others deferred to Stokes, who looked to be the youngest of the group. They chatted like old friends as they made their way up the Lawn and exited around the Rotunda.

They didn't talk to him and he didn't try to make conversation. Any casual observer might think that the five were traveling together, nothing amiss. These men were definitely pros. Price had no doubt that if he made a break for freedom one or all of the men would have easily incapacitated him, especially the quiet one with the pony tail. Something in his eyes screamed professional. Hell, they all did. And yet, he didn't get the feeling that these were cruel men, men Cromwell might hire. Strange.

Price decided to bide his time and see what would happen.

———

CAL HAD observed Price on the way back to their new headquarters, watching for any signs that the man was wavering on their accord. The man seemed lost in thought. Hell, Cal didn't blame the guy. More than anything, Cal couldn't shake the feeling that despite his earlier posturing, Price seemed relieved, like a man who'd been through hell and back and finally got a chance at a sip of water.

After dodging the workers in the backyard who were busy installing a full outdoor entertainment area, courtesy of Jonas, they were greeted in the kitchen by the rest of the team, arranged casually in the dining area and on the chairs in the living area. They were operators who'd seen all manner of good and evil in their travels. Few things spooked them and even fewer made them stare in awe. But that's what happened when Price walked in the door. They all wanted to know the same thing, whether or not this doctor was, in fact, the key to the cure for one of the world's most deadly diseases.

Their number made Price hesitate, pausing at the door. Cal ignored the nervous look on his face and asked, "Can I get you something to drink, Doc? Water? Beer?"

Price nodded and stepped inside. "Do you have anything stronger?"

There were chuckles from the rest of the men, Cal among them.

"Sure. Whiskey. Bourbon. Vodka..."

"Whiskey, please. Neat."

Cal smiled and fetched the drink for their guest. Dr. Price downed it in one swig and handed it back to Cal.

"Another?" asked Cal, eyebrow raised.

"Please."

———

THEY CONVENED in the War Room. Cal asked Dr. Higgins to join them. It never hurt to have the master of the human psyche in attendance. The others scattered around the room included Daniel, Trent, Jonas, Gaucho and Neil.

Jonas was almost giddy, still having a hard time believing that his hunch had nabbed the interesting specimen who now sat nursing his third drink. "You've got to tell us, Dr. Price, is it for real? Are you really healing people?"

A sip and a nod later, Price said, "It's true."

Silence in the room. They'd been talking about it since Jonas had floated his crazy idea. All eyes were on the mysterious Dr. Price.

"How did you do it?" asked Neil, leaning closer just like his friends.

Price didn't answer at first, his hesitation apparent despite his alcohol-coaxed calm. Finally, he sat his drink on the conference table, folded his arms across his chest and began his tale.

———

THREE YEARS EARLIER, Price was in the middle of containing four separate Ebola outbreaks in Africa. It was his team who was sending much needed medicine and staff to assist local officials. Dr. Price had already made seven trips himself.

It was at the end of an exhausting Friday that one of his assistants came to him with a shot in the dark.

"Dr. Price, I know you probably don't have time for this, but I thought I'd put it in your inbox."

Price kept an open door policy with his staff, always encouraging them to be creative and experiment on their own. He'd found that option to be rare in the confines of government funding, but his time with the SEALs had taught him the value of individual initiative coupled with a strong team dynamic.

"I'll take a look at it this weekend, Sheila. Why don't you tell the others to head on out. I'm about to leave myself."

It was a white lie and Sheila knew it. Dr. Price rarely left the office before 9pm. There was always some new outbreak to look after or a lead on a cure.

After making the rounds through the confines of his small domain, gently prodding his staff to go home for the night, Price headed back into his paper-strewn office, taking in the mess the week had rained down on his once orderly second home. He was tempted to lie down on the olive drab military cot in the corner, but grabbed another cup of coffee instead and decided to attack his inbox. It was overflowing as usual, so he did what he always did: started from the top.

He made quick work of the thin report Sheila had submitted, wondering at first why she'd brought it to his attention. It had nothing to do with infectious disease, making it outside their purview. Nevertheless, Price read through the interesting notes, impressed by the connections. She had a flair for storytelling, and this was no exception.

Price looked up from the report and closed his eyes. He

didn't have time for fantasy, but Sheila's conclusions were intriguing, if a bit farfetched. In her concise abstract she'd given a brief history of an obscure tribe of natives living in a dense region of the Amazon rainforest in south-eastern Colombia.

According to Sheila, the area had one of the lowest per capita rates of cancer in the world. That interested Dr. Price, not because of the articles outlining superstitious rumors and old wives' tales referenced by the talented author, but because of the raw data she'd provided. Reports from traveling missionaries and reputable health organizations. The occasional census by Colombia's government. And yet, no one had ever made more than a passing note of the extremely low incidence of cancer among the population. They'd never connected the dots.

Sheila thought along the same lines as Price, hypothesizing that no one had ever taken a moment to step back and gather the correct information. They were too busy feeding the hungry or providing much needed medical care to orphans and the impoverished. Or worse, fighting the constant battle against narco-traffickers.

Dr. Price sat back and let the first inkling of possibility seep in. It wasn't time to alert his superiors. They wanted concrete evidence, results to back up his team's assumptions. Price yawned into his hand and glanced at his calendar. He had some leave time coming, and he'd just earned another grant, a portion of which could easily support a small expedition down to South America.

TWO WEEKS LATER, Dr. Price, Sheila and a three-man security team hopped a commercial flight from Washington, D.C. to Bogota, Colombia. From there they boarded another plane bound for Alfredo Vasquez Cobo International Airport, located in Colombia's most southern city of Leticia. Price hadn't told his boss the true nature of the trip, still not convinced that the stories were real. Instead, he'd submitted the request citing an increased need for local contacts in the region that could source potentially life-saving resources from the Amazon basin.

Leticia's location made things a bit complicated, mostly because the city sat on the border of Brazil, and was at the tip of the cocaine pipeline, hence the added security.

Luckily for Price, the trip down proved uneventful. He found the Colombians to be gracious hosts and it seemed as though they'd made major progress in their battle against the drug cartels. Or maybe it was a happy truce after the heavy bloodshed of the 1990s. Either way, they reached Leticia without incident, their local guide waiting in the hotel lobby as they entered.

They left the next morning in their guide's mud spattered Toyota Landcruiser. More than once Price had wished he'd brought a mouth guard what with the near constant jostling as Antonio sped them toward their destination. Finally, after almost six hours of driving, they unloaded their gear and stepped into the rain forest. Price had never been to South America except on vacation, and the sheer grandeur of the place enticed his senses. It made him feel alive. Sounds he'd never heard called from all around. Smells both fresh and damp mingled in the humid air.

Where others might have been overwhelmed by the heat and the oppression under the tree canopy, Price marveled at the greenery, the flecks of bright color here and there, from lichen and animals alike.

Antonio led the way, guided by the worn GPS Price was sure had a whole roll of duct tape keeping it together. It didn't seem to worry their guide, who picked his way effort-lessly through the tangle.

Two hours of trudging got them to their first destination, one of three known camps used by the tribe they were looking for. They were all soaked as they made their way to the center of the small village. Crude huts made from roughly cut tree branches and covered in foliage made a ring around the fire pit in the middle.

No one was there.

"Where are they?" Price asked their guide.

"Maybe hunting, señor. We wait and see," said Antonio.

Apparently the entire tribe usually went out on daily hunting parties, the men doing the finding, and the women and children doing the prepping on the way back to camp. Antonio said by the looks of the camp he might have picked the correct location.

"How do you know?" asked Sheila.

Antonio just shrugged and took a long drink from a bottle of orange soda.

They got their answer just as the sun was setting three hours later. The first warriors, if you could call them that, sauntered into camp, unperturbed by the presence of strangers, wearing an assortment of tattered rags, all barefoot, bare-chested and a full foot shorter than the Americans. The tribe scattered to their chores as Antonio struck up a conversation with the fattest man of the bunch who wore what looked like the large teeth of some predator in each ear.

He gestured with his hands and jabbered on in a dialect that Price couldn't pinpoint. Spanish? Portuguese? The man kept pointing to the jungle, back the way they'd come.

Antonio came back to join his charges. "He says the medicine man that way." He pointed the same way the chieftain had.

"Why isn't he with the rest of the tribe?" asked Price.

"Gathering," answered Antonio, already picking up his belongings and heading for the skinny dirt path.

They found the stick thin medicine man no more than thirty minutes later, the tinkling of small bones and hollow sticks knocking against a walking stick he used as he headed toward them. He had a sack slung over his shoulder, the leaves of his harvest peeking out over the lip.

He stopped when he noticed the strangers approaching. Squinting as if getting confirmation of something he'd just seen, the medicine man's eyes went wide and his cragged finger pointed directly at Dr. Price. The tribe elder muttered something Price didn't understand.

"What did he say?" Price asked their guide.

Antonio shook his head and asked the man to repeat himself. Their guide's face twisted in confusion.

"What did he say?" Price asked again.

"He say you finally come."

"Who? Us?"

"No, Doctor. He say you."

The medicine man moved closer, shuffling with a slight limp as he made his way to Price, who could smell him well before the native stood in front of him. It wasn't an unpleasant smell, more of a mixture of unknown herbs and earth.

Stepping right up to Price, the man reached up and traced half circles under Price's eyes, muttering something again. Price looked to Antonio for the translation.

"He say you *The Traveler*, señor."

CHARLOTTESVILLE, VIRGINIA

I t was like someone had sucked all the air out of the room. Not a man moved, latched onto Price's story.

The good doctor knew his skill as an orator, something years of forced practice as a kid molded without much thought. It felt good to tell someone what he knew. For some reason he believed with all his heart that he could trust these men. The looks in their eyes told of goodness and heroism. Just as they were sucked in by his retelling, he too was relaxing after months on the run.

"Next thing I knew the old native grabbed me by the hand and led me farther down the path, motioning for the others to stay put. I didn't come out for two days."

"Where did he take you?" asked Gaucho.

"He had a little hut deeper in the jungle. From our rudimentary communication I picked up that he never brought anyone else. It was weird and I don't really know how to explain it, but he treated me like an equal, open with his basic instruction. Kinda like he was training a pupil to take over for him."

"And he showed you his secret?" asked Jonas.

"He did. The cure was made out of some kind of root. He never showed me where he got it. I think that maybe it was a seasonal thing. Anyway, he'd make a sort of a poultice out of it, grinding it up and making it into paste then setting it out in the sun. All the villagers ate it as part of their diet because it took a constant active supply to suppress the cancer," Price explained.

"How does it work?" asked Neil, obviously intrigued by the potential.

"Most people don't know that there are over one hundred diseases that are lumped under the cancer umbrella. Traditionally, cancer research focused on killing off the abnormal cells. Chemotherapy and radiation are the most common. The medicine man's supplement did something else completely. I didn't know it until I took a sample back to my lab, but instead of killing off the cancerous cells, the medicine actually helped the cancer integrate into the host tissue. Instead of invading and taking it over, it played nice and latched on like a friend. Eventually the cell became part of whatever organ it had at first invaded."

"Hold on. You just said that the villagers supplemented their diets with this stuff. Are you saying the drug you snuck around giving people is going to wear off?" asked Cal.

Price smiled, expecting the question. "No. I was able to engineer the medicine man's stuff into something stronger. Call it an immunization just like the polio vaccine. But unlike a traditional vaccine where we use viral particles or dead viruses to trigger a reaction, this substance is more like a salve. It's like it soothes the agitated cancer cells into playing nice and then fully integrating."

"You're fucking kidding me," said a visibly shocked Cal. The rest of the room mirrored his look.

"Nope. I can give the vaccine intravenously, with a simple shot, even orally, and that's it. As long as a patient's body hasn't been completely ravaged by the cancer, my success rate is one hundred percent."

———

WASHINGTON, D.C. - 12:30PM, APRIL 6TH

The Senate Subcommittee on Labor, Health, Human Services, Education and Related Agencies was subordinate to the highly visible Senate Appropriations Committee. While not as powerful as its big brother, the Subcommittee had recently gained more clout with the passage of the Affordable Care Act. With the overhaul of the American healthcare system a continuing drain for Democrats and Republicans alike, the chairman of the newly spotlighted subcommittee was once again on the rise within the senate chambers. While not specifically overseeing the healthcare change, the group's jurisdiction over entities like the National Institute of Health, the centers for Medicare and Medicaid Services and Centers for Disease Control and Prevention afforded obvious parallels and overlap. Simply put, the Affordable Care Act had a direct effect on the subcommittee's oversight.

Senator Mac Thompson, the subcommittee's chairman, banged his gavel, sounding the end of the day's session, another round of endless droning by a handful of lobbyists looking for more money. Sen. Thompson had only half listened to the testimony, his mind elsewhere.

"How's your son doing, Mac?" asked Senator Alphonse Pontre, a swarthy Hawaiian with a gleaming smile.

"He's doing much better. Thanks for asking, Al," said Thompson.

"They taking good care of him at Georgetown?"

"They are. Good crew up there."

"Good. Please let me know if I can do anything, okay?" Sen. Pontre patted his friend on the back, giving Thompson that knowing look, the same one he'd gotten from anyone who'd had any exposure to cancer. It was the "poor bastard" look.

Thompson knew it wasn't intentional, they were only trying to be helpful, but it burned him up inside. He'd show them, every fucking one of them, dammit.

Ignoring the calls from the gallery, Thompson made a quick exit through the senate chambers and out to the car that was waiting curbside. He was anxious to get his son's results.

"Hey, Dad! I didn't know you were coming by today," said Michael Thompson when his father strode into the room with an armful of magazines. He set his load on the table next to the bed and gave his son a hug. The senator wasn't sure if it was just hope, but Michael looked better. More color.

"Are you kidding? I wanted to be here when the doctors give you your update. Besides, couldn't have you lying around without the latest *Sport Illustrated*. There's a great article in there about the National's new pitcher.

Michael smiled. He looked stronger too. Something in his eyes. "Thanks, Dad. Have you eaten yet?"

"I ordered on the way in. They should have it here in a second. So, tell me what I missed."

Father and son spent lunch trading stories. Michael filled the senator in on the latest news from baseball's spring training reports, something they'd traveled to for years, all except this year. Thompson told his son about the lobbyist who'd obviously had too much to drink the night before, and had almost passed out mid-sentence after turning a swamp-colored green. Michael laughed at his father's retelling, the sound alone filling his father with hope.

All too soon not one but five doctors entered the private room. Sen. Thompson turned their way, trying to read the expressions on the physicians' faces.

"Good morning, Senator. Good morning, Michael," said Michael's oncologist, Dr. Mehta, a middle aged Indian woman who'd come highly recommended from friends.

Thompson nodded, unable to find the saliva to answer, his mouth suddenly parched.

"Hey, Doc. Are you here to tell me I'm being released today?" asked Michael, his boyish features smiling with the same look he'd had since birth.

Dr. Mehta looked uncomfortable, like she was about to deliver bad news. Sen. Thompson's chest clenched.

"We'd like to run a few tests in order to—" Dr. Mehta started.

"What did you find, Doctor?" Sen. Thompson finally found his voice, wanting to know. The strength in his tone shook the normally resolute Dr. Mehta.

"I...it's not necessarily bad news, Senator. I..."

"Then let's have it, doctor." Thompson's heart raced. He was already planning for contingencies, dealing with Cromwell, finding other options...

He felt a hand on his arm. It was Michael's. "Come on, Dad. Let her talk." Michael smiled at his doctor, prompting her to continue. Sen. Thompson felt like exploding.

"It's just that...well, I've been very open with you both from the beginning," said Dr. Mehta. "I promise I'll continue that for as long as you're under my care."

Why won't this bitch just tell us? I knew I should've used that other guy at Mayo, thought Sen. Thompson.

"I won't bore you with the details yet, but it seems that your blood cell counts have somewhat normalized. The most recent readings also show that your persistent fever has dropped, as have several of your other nagging symptoms. Tell me, Michael, how are you feeling?"

"I feel better than I have in months. No puking's a big bonus."

Dr. Mehta looked to her colleagues, who all wore similar looks of puzzlement.

They all thought my son was going to die.

"I'll have the tech take some more samples and we'll schedule you for a full work-up. We should know more by tomorrow," said Mehta.

Senator Mac Thompson ignored the doctors as they said their goodbyes, instead turning to his son, tears already in his eyes. He put a delicate hand to his son's cheek and brought him closer, holding him as the emotion of relief flowed uncontrolled.

"Jeez, Dad. You okay?"

Thompson moved so they were now forehead to forehead, the closeness something the elder Thompson needed. "We're gonna be okay, son. We're gonna be okay."

CHARLOTTESVILLE, VIRGINIA

They'd spent almost two hours peppering Dr. Price with questions, trying to come to grips with what they'd heard. It was as if God had sent Jesus back to Earth and they were there to witness it. Gaucho made the sign of the cross more than once. Jonas kept mumbling to himself, something about the possibilities and the impact on the world. Daniel sat with a look of utter tranquility, as if to say "I told you so" to the world he'd come to view with a more enlightened sense of being.

Cal was the only one who still seemed rooted to reality. While he appreciated the revelation, he was still very concerned about why Price was doing it on his own. Where was his staff? Who had funded the research? Cal had allowed his team to ask their questions first, following the old Marine Corps system of allowing the most junior to chime in before their leaders. He'd gotten better at it since joining SSI, tempering his emotions once he realized the importance of allowing each team member the chance to ask questions or submit their own recommendations. Cal had found that the system worked, often allowing him to reconsider his initial thoughts and devise a better game plan as a result.

So after everyone had their chance to ask Price about the villagers, Colombia, the intricacies of his research, and his time on the road, his men looked to him. It was their leader's turn.

"You still haven't told us why you're doing this, Doctor Price. Why you and why all by yourself?" asked Cal.

Price considered the question, obviously hesitant with a response.

"That's a question with a very complicated answer."

"We've got time," said Cal, crossing his arms across his chest. Now they were getting somewhere, to the meat of it.

Again the hesitation from Price, but with averted eyes, he said, "Like I said, it's a long story, but the long and the short of it is that I am a fugitive."

"So you stole the cure?" asked Cal.

"Yes and no," said Price, the struggle to explain evident in his tone.

"Who are you running from?"

Price explained his background, his time with the SEALs, the time spent overseas and his last assignment with the National Institutes of Health and his collaboration with the CDC.

"Not long after my team and I perfected the vaccine, things changed. One of my lead researchers was reassigned to Atlanta, another got an obscure grant she'd submitted ten years before while in grad school. Pretty soon it was just me. They kept telling me that replacements were on the way but none came. Honestly, I noticed it, but I didn't. The implications of my research had consumed me to such a level that I rarely left the office, never made time for friends and almost never saw my family. I'd shut myself in, disconnected from the world I'd promised to help. My work consumed me until it was too late."

"What happened?" asked Cal.

"One morning, after returning from a forced vacation with my family, I got back to the office and noticed that certain things were out of place. We had a housekeeping staff member who would occasionally put things out of place, but something felt different. Maybe it was the fact that I'd finally gotten a decent week's rest. Whatever it was, I started looking around. Sure enough, I found that certain files had been tampered with. Early on I'd had the wherewithal to load a tracking program on my collection of work computers. I wanted to make sure no one was tampering with my files. It was pretty basic and probably why it wasn't noticed. Rather than keep people out, it simply recorded changes made and unique logins. With the push of a button I could pull up a report. That morning I ran the report and found that my files had been accessed multiple times while I was away."

"Did the files technically belong to you?" asked Cal, familiar with the way government agencies worked within the realm of "need to know."

"Not technically, but other than my former staff and myself, no one had ever attempted to access those files. I was given autonomy and people rarely asked for anything as long as my team produced. This was blatant. This was someone trying to take my research."

"Did you tell your boss?"

"Not right away. One of the few smart things I did was to make a copy of the most important data and formulations. I hid them away just in case someone tried to go around me. I'm lucky I did. When I got around to telling my boss, he gave me some line about routine software updates and security sweeps. Someone else might have believed him, but my antenna was way up by that point. After that day, I didn't confide in him more than I was required to."

"So you find out someone's snooping on you, you've got no team and your boss is lying to you. What made you jump off the deep end?" asked Cal.

Price exhaled, his energy suddenly drained.

"One morning I showed up to work and a crew was packing up all my things. My boss was right there with them, so I asked him what was going on. He said that the program was being handed to a senior team in another department who'd be in charge of the implementation. I was being shipped off to London for some collaborative tour. To say that I was irate is an understatement. I wanted to deck him right there, but I held my tongue and my fist."

"And?"

"I did the only thing I could think of. Apparently they hadn't rescinded my security clearance yet. They also hadn't relocated the live vaccines. It was just a matter of walking down to the lab and throwing a few in my backpack along with some of my personal belongings. They didn't even search me when I left. I guess they didn't think I was that big of a threat."

There were chuckles from the others. Even Cal smiled. "I guess they learned their lesson."

Price nodded. "I never went back. I found out later that a bunch of black masked guys descended on my house hours later. Got that tidbit from a neighbor who decided to email me to see if I was okay. I shuffled my money around as quickly as I could. Anything I hadn't moved was confiscated in a matter of hours."

"Where did you go?" asked Cal.

"I found a crappy little motel, paid with cash, and hunkered down for a week. The fourth night there I happened to be surfing the web when the Google alert I'd set up with my name popped up in my email. It was a brief article based on a press report issued by the CDC. It said that I'd been killed in a mugging. Body found on the banks of the Potomac. Christ, the reporter had even contacted my family who'd just heard of the accident. He said they were planning the funeral service for later that week."

By then there were tears in Price's eyes. He looked like what he was, a man who'd lost everything. Cal could sympathize. He'd not only lost his parents, but then later his fiancé to a crazy gangster. More than the story of the cure, the fact that Price had been wronged in such an egregious way made Cal want to fight for the man.

"Last question and then we'll grab some lunch," said Cal.

Price looked up, wiping the tears from his eyes with his shirt sleeve. "Sure."

"What was your old boss's name?"

Price's eyes hardened and he sat a little bit straighter.

"Cromwell. Colonel Gormon Cromwell."

NATIONAL INSTITUTES OF HEALTH HEADQUARTERS

BETHESDA, MARYLAND - 2:19PM, APRIL 6TH

Col. Cromwell told his secretary to hold all calls and to reschedule his afternoon meetings. He needed time to think, time to reorganize. The latest report from his scientists was not promising. They were no closer to replicating Dr. Price's work. To make matters worse, they were down to their last vial of the starter agent. He'd hoped to either have his overpaid brains come up with a copy of the vaccine, or have Price under his control to do it himself.

While there were still plenty of funds left at his disposal, the money men were getting anxious. They wanted results and they wanted them now. Cromwell wasn't used to having people breathing down his neck. He'd lasted as long as he had because of his reputation and the fact that most people left him alone. Those who didn't either found themselves without a job, reassigned to Alaska or worse.

But Hunter Price was the problem that just wouldn't go away. They'd been so close to nabbing him on more than one occasion. He couldn't fault his trusted Malik Vespers. The man was an enforcer, not a tracker. Cromwell was the one who fed Vespers the information and the silent sentinel then rode off to demolish whatever obstacle was in his way. More eunuch than bodyguard, the man was an immovable object, never having failed to serve his master.

Cromwell let his eyes roam, taking in the pictures of death and pestilence, destruction cast down by incurable disease, abject poverty and the sheer evil of man. His gaze lingered on one picture, remembering the time and place, once again smelling the putridity of rotting corpses. It made him smile. He had his answer.

————

CHARLOTTESVILLE, VIRGINIA

Daniel picked up the War Room telephone.

"Yes, sir. He's right here." He motioned to Cal. "It's Brandon."

Cal nodded and took the phone. "What's up Mister President?"

"I know this is last minute, but I was wondering if you could run by the Charlottesville airport and say hello. We'll be touching down in twenty minutes."

"Perfect timing. It just so happens that I have an update for you," said Cal.

"Wanna give me a hint?" asked the president.

"I think it'll be better if I tell you in person. See you in twenty."

Cal hung up the phone and turned to Dr. Price, who was just finishing his lunch, a nuclear sub from Little John's Deli. He'd torn it apart like a starving orphan. "Hey, Doc. You ready to see the president?"

TWENTY MINUTES LATER, Air Force One landed, effectively shutting down all traffic in and out of the Charlottesville Airport. The crew and their Secret Service counterparts knew the havoc caused by a presidential landing and were careful not to overstay their welcome. The good news was that they weren't landing in a major hub like Atlanta or Los Angeles.

As soon as the stairs were wheeled to the huge aircraft's door, Cal, Dr. Price, Daniel and MSgt Trent ran up the steps even as the portal opened.

The president was waiting inside his office wearing a relaxed golf outfit over his fit and recently tanned body. Cal had been through a lot with Brandon Zimmer, and he'd had his doubts about the democrat's abilities, but over the past months he'd come to view the good-looking politician as someone who looked and acted like a president.

Price stood to the side and the others greeted the president with a mix of handshakes and hugs. These men were friends of the president, not just acquaintances.

Zimmer smiled and extended his hand after escaping MSgt Trent's bear hug. "Brandon Zimmer."

"It's a pleasure, Mr. President. Doctor Hunter Price, sir."

"I'd love to know what you're doing hanging out with these misfits, Dr. Price. Is Cal finally having his head checked out?"

Price's eyebrow's rose as Zimmer threw his friends a wink. He obviously didn't know what to say.

"Don't listen to him, Doc. The president's just as big of a misfit as the rest of us," said MSgt Trent, patting Price on the back.

Price nodded, but didn't say anything.

Zimmer turned back to Cal. "Does Dr. Price have something to do with what you wanted to tell me?"

"He does."

"Let's take a seat and you can fill me in on what you've been up to."

It took Cal two minutes to get Zimmer up to date on what they'd accomplished with their new dual headquarters and finding viable missions. Ten minutes later he'd detailed the search for Dr. Price and the naval officer's incredible story.

Zimmer had heard all manner of story since entering politics, but the fact that a cure for cancer had supposedly been found seemed to top them all.

"And you're sure this is a permanent fix, doctor?" asked Zimmer.

"Yes, sir. While the data is still young, every patient I've dosed has yet to relapse. No degradation. I'm sure the vaccine will work for the lifetime of the person."

Zimmer shook his head. "This is…incredible."

"There's the problem of this Colonel Cromwell," said Cal. "What do you want us to do about him?"

"Travis is staying in D.C. while I fly out to Seattle for a day. I'll have him make some discreet inquiries. Until then, I think you should do what you can to secure the material you need to duplicate the vaccine."

Travis Haden was Cal's first cousin and former CEO of Stokes Security International. The former SEAL was almost as big of a smart ass as Cal and now served as Zimmer's chief of staff, a reluctant choice he'd quickly grown to excel at. There weren't many people Cal trusted more than Travis. The last thing he needed was Cromwell getting any whiff of them looking into his background. Travis would know how to handle it.

"Okay. Do we have your permission to go out of the country?" asked Cal.

"Where to?"

"Colombia. I think we need to get our hands on that

medicine man before Cromwell does. If I were him, the first thing I'd do was secure the source."

Zimmer thought about it for a moment then said, "Do what you need to, but you know the drill. Low profile. We won't need to piss off the Colombians. They've got enough on their plate right now."

Cal smiled. "You got it."

ENROUTE TO LETICIA, COLOMBIA

7:25PM, APRIL 7TH

Dr. Price couldn't believe how quickly Cal's team saddled up for their expedition to Colombia. Not only did the former Marine have the ear and consent of the president of the United States, he also apparently commanded enough clout to charter a National Guard KC-130 for transport. The pilot looked like a kid except for his blazing yellow handlebar mustache. Everyone else knew him. He introduced himself as Cowboy. It was an appropriate call sign considering the matching cowboy hat and blaring country music as they departed Andrew Air Force Base.

While not exactly eager to fly out of the country, Price knew the trip would have to happen at some point. Better to go with a group of warriors than on his own. He'd tried to plan an excursion to South America months before, but without appropriate identification or means of travel he was literally stranded in his home country. Not that it was a huge issue, but if he wanted to produce more of the vaccine, a trip south was necessary. If only he'd had the access to the starter serum when he'd left!

He looked around at the men he'd hoped would help him on his quest and to regain his old life. Much like his time with the SEALs, some of them slept, others chatted over the drone of the military aircraft and the rest played cards or read. It was like coming home. It felt familiar being amongst such men.

Determined to be prepared before landing, Price went back to the notes he'd started extracting from his brain. That, along with his knowledge of the area, would be vital in the coming days. He did not want to let these men down. They might only have one chance.

———

THEY TOUCHED DOWN IN LETICIA, Colombia without incident. Despite Gaucho's assurances to the contrary, Cal half expected a delegation of Colombian drug lords or FARC soldiers to be waiting. That didn't happen. Instead, a kind and stately looking gentleman named Augusto escorted them through customs with a wave of his hand. Their path had been paved in dollar bills.

Founded as a Peruvian port in 1867, the small city of Leticia was annexed by Colombia in 1922 after their war with Peru. Sitting at the corner of the drug smuggling world, bordering Peru and Brazil, the one-time haven of smugglers and adventurers alike now seemed to be reborn. Cal had never been to Colombia, but Gaucho had. He'd given the rest of the team a briefing on the area.

Located more than 500 miles from Colombia's main highway, the main ways in and out of Leticia were by plane or by boat on the Amazon River. Gaucho had instructed his fellow operators to keep their mouths shut and eyes and ears open.

Although the area was relatively tame compared to the lawless '80s and '90s, criminal elements still had a firm grip on the area. It would be inevitable that they would be seen, but money went a long way in Colombia. Public officials and criminals alike were used to turning a blind eye as long as they were allowed to wet their beaks with cold hard cash.

And so it was that Cal's team, led by the aristocratic Augusto, made their way to a muddy grouping of late model Toyota 4x4s and piled in.

THEY GOT to their initial destination without incident. No tails. No surveillance that any of them could see. Augusto had chatted in his nasal clip, extolling the many fine qualities of "The New Colombia" and the growing economy of Leticia. Cal wondered how much of the growth was attributed to the cocaine trade.

"This is it." Dr. Price pointed to a spot ahead marked by two fallen trees.

The team got out of the vehicles warily, weapons trained on the surrounding tree line, its gigantic trees casting shadows across the dirt road. Without prompting, Gaucho's men secured the perimeter while Cal, Daniel, MSgt Trent and Dr. Price took a look at Price's sketches.

"I'll take point," said Daniel.

While Cal would've rather had the sniper by his side, he knew the best place for Daniel was in the shadows. His uncanny luck and sixth sense were invaluable.

"Okay. Doc, I want you in the middle of the pack. Me and Top will follow Daniel with a couple of Gaucho's guys. Any questions?" asked Cal.

There were none.

Two minutes later they stepped off, pacing into the

steamy jungle as their host remained behind with two of Cal's men, just in case.

THE JUNGLE WAS EERILY QUIET, making the hairs all over Daniel's body stand straight up. He could sense that something wasn't right in the mugginess of midday. Sniffing the air for confirmation, Daniel moved ahead, careful to move slowly down the exposed path.

Coming around the bend, he was hit by a face full of flies. He tried to swat them away, continuing his forward movement. The insects must have decided there were easier targets close by and flew off. Rounding a slight bend, alarm bells rang in Daniel's head.

When the clearing finally appeared, he took in the scene with a detached eye, still scanning for threats. Even as he did so he said a silent prayer for the carrion-covered dead crucified in the blood-streaked trees surrounding the empty village.

COLOMBIAN JUNGLE

1:19PM, APRIL 8TH

After securing the area, the team set about taking the villagers down from the trees. Children. Wives. Fathers. All dead. All told, there were over fifty murdered villagers, many with their insides, eyes and tender portions already torn out by animals and insects.

Cal's men methodically stacked the bodies. Most had done this horrid duty before. Men of honor abhorred such atrocity and to a man they hoped to put their hands on, or better yet a bullet through, the murderers who'd descended on the peaceful village.

Dr. Price found it hard to help, tears streaming as he went about the gruesome task of removing the natives from their hanging perches. He blamed himself. If he'd never set foot in the village, the death of the kind Indians never would have happened.

Price searched the bodies, looking for the wrinkled medicine man who'd called him "The Traveler." Frantic to find him, Price's breathing came in gasps. After making a full circle around the upturned bodies, he looked up.

"He's not here."

AFTER SETTING the bodies on fire and leaving two more men to guard their way back, Daniel led the way farther down the path in search of the missing shaman. Jaws set to match their resolve, the warriors crept on.

THEY FOUND the medicine man much as they had his fellow villagers. The only difference was that instead of being nailed to the wide tree with his hands and feet, the medicine man had two foot-long railroad stakes nailed through his eyes, his heart and his groin. There was also a crude sign nailed to the tree above his head. It said, "Diablo," Devil in Spanish.

As Price rushed to the old man's hut, fire erupted from their flank, taking down two of their number.

Like the trained professionals they were, Cal's men took cover and returned disciplined fire, even the wounded. You could hardly see a thing through the undergrowth, except for the occasional muzzle flash. Then came the RPG rounds.

Cal directed the men to move forward, seeing one of his men take a hit in the shoulder. The experienced operator shook it off and kept moving, firing and maneuvering as he went.

More rounds flew overhead and more explosions sounded as repeated RPG rounds slammed into the trees above them. Poor aim, but still deadly should someone get lucky with a shot.

Daniel was nowhere in sight. He'd disappeared. Cal knew the sniper was doing what he did best, finding the enemy.

From the gunfire Cal estimated that there were at least twenty enemy fighters and they didn't appear to be closing in, instead maintaining cover. Sensing it before it actually happened, Cal threw himself to the side just as another RPG round slammed into the tree next to where he'd been standing, sending Cal flying, the creeping darkness already swallowing him.

DANIEL COULDN'T BELIEVE he hadn't seen the ambush coming. Cool anger fueled his movement as he sprinted his way through the jungle, trusting God and his instincts to keep him safe. If he didn't get to the enemy soon more of his friends would die. He couldn't let that happen.

Plowing ahead, a ghost in his element, Snake Eyes closed in, his inner beast unleashed.

RAUL NADIN WAS on his fifth magazine, the rounds going quickly. He'd opted to stick his AK-47 above his head and over the log he was hiding behind, squeezing the trigger. To hell with aiming. He didn't want to die. He wasn't getting paid enough money for what he'd done in the last day. It wasn't that he necessarily felt remorse over what they'd done to the Amazonian tribe, they were Godless heathens after all, but Raul didn't want to die.

Only twenty-one years of age, Raul hoped to marry within the month, and he needed money, not to mention his life, to do it. Loading another magazine into his weapon, Raul lifted the barrel over the sturdy log even as he noticed a shadow to the side. He turned, confused. He was on the far right flank. Shrugging when he didn't see anything to confirm his suspicions, he went to lift his weapon again only to find that it was no longer in his hands.

Then the pain hit as he raised his arms, bloody geyser stumps spraying his lifeblood like the burst pipe at his grandmother's house. A man crouched next to him. He had just enough time to make out the man's eyes and the crimson dripping machete in his hand as the blade swept in, finishing the deed.

———

CAL WOKE to MSgt Trent shaking him, his ears ringing.

"Cal, you okay?"

"What?"

His vision was blurry, but his other senses were returning. Except for a raging headache and a few soon-to-be bruises, he felt whole.

"I'm good."

Cal could barely hear his own voice, but took Trent's hand and hefted himself back to his feet. Rather than babysit his friend, Trent took off in the direction of the firing. Cal followed right behind.

———

HALF of the Colombian line had fallen silent before their commander, a chubby thirty-something with an eye patch and a hair-lip, noticed that anything was amiss.

Fuckers better not be running away. He growled to himself.

Unafraid of death, he moved to see what the problem was. He'd picked out the position personally, knowing a fair amount about infantry tactics from his time as a sergeant in the Colombian army.

His boss had given him a score of untrained troops,

promising him a big payday when he succeeded. He didn't care about his troops being killed. That meant more money in his pocket, but if any of the idiots ran off, he would find them and kill them personally.

The first sign that something was wrong was when he found his most seasoned man, an aged foulmouth from Bogota, with his decapitated head lying next to his body. His body froze, everything coming into stark focus. He realized the only firing he heard was from his own men. The telltale feel of rounds overhead were no longer coming. As if in slow motion, he whirled around to face the menace at his back. He was met with curved blade arching toward his face.

———

CAL KNEW how Daniel worked and left him to his task, ensuring that the rest of his men held their fire. Something told him that he would know when to press the attack. They still moved forward, but more cautiously. He felt the tide turning. Fewer rounds coming, more empty space to move.

Suddenly a blood-curdling scream sounded from ahead, followed by the cessation of most of the automatic weapons. Without hesitating, Cal sprinted out of his crouch and charged.

———

MOST OF THE work was already done by the time the rest of the team got there. Cal took down two with his pistol. Trent another with his own. Others had neatly placed head shots from earlier. The rest of the men secured a hasty perimeter under Gaucho's direction.

They found Daniel searching the bodies of the dead. All

alone, the deadly sniper had dispatched twelve men with a fucking machete. He'd brought it along just in case.

Cal shook his head, wincing at the pain in the side of his neck. That was going to be sore.

"Thanks for saving some for us," he said.

Daniel didn't stop his search.

"I've got one over there. I think he's their leader," said Daniel without looking up.

Cal moved to where Daniel pointed, finding a paunchy guy in a stretched pinstriped button down and a patch over one eye. He looked like an overweight pirate. Cal nudged him with his boot. The man stirred, his eyes fluttering open.

Fat pirate went to grab his weapon that was no longer in his grasp.

"Don't move," said Cal, his pistol aimed at the man's face. "Gaucho, come talk to this guy."

ONCE HE SAW how completely his force had been decimated, the fat pirate started talking. The order had been passed down from his boss much like any other mission. They'd killed the villagers and lain in wait for a follow-on force. Ordered to stay in place for at least two days, the mercenaries were told that bringing back some alive would earn them a bonus, but that killing them was all that was needed.

The guy didn't have a clue why they were doing it, just that they'd get paid. He relaxed more and more, realizing that Cal and his men were not cold blooded murderers and that they were probably some kind of soldiers. Soldiers, especially American soldiers, drew the line at killing captives. By the end of the story the man was talking to Gaucho like an old friend, smiling like an idiot.

"Tell him he's coming with us," said Cal.

Gaucho delivered the news while Cal talked to Daniel and

MSgt Trent. "I wanna get out of here fast. There's nothing we can do."

Just then Dr. Price walked up to the group, still looking a bit shaken. "But we need to find what we came for."

"No way, Doc. Too dangerous. It's getting dark and I'm not sticking around this shithole any longer than I have to."

"Give me a couple minutes to look around the shaman's hut," pleaded Price.

"Fine. You've got five minutes then we go."

THEY COULDN'T FIND anything of use in the old man's hut. Price begged for more time, but Cal denied the request. "We've got the coordinates from our GPS. Once we get things settled back home you can come down here with a bigger party and search for as long as you want." Cal started toward the path.

"But—"

Cal whirled around. "Our mission was to find the medicine man, not to get in a firefight with a drug lord's troops. I've got six men who need medical attention. Feel free to stay out here if you want, but we're heading out."

Price was torn. "Okay." He slipped in behind one of the wounded men and followed the extraction the way they'd come.

THE TEAM HAD ALMOST REACHED the village when Daniel signaled for a halt. His inner alarm clanged. There was someone watching them.

Cal moved up to join him. "What's up?"

Daniel gestured with a circular motion. "We're being watched."

As the last word came out of Daniel's mouth, a diminutive

native stepped out of the jungle without a sound, carrying a crude spear sharpened at one end. He stood in the middle of the path. Daniel lowered his weapon and motioned for the others to do the same.

"Hey, Doc, you wanna come up here?" said Cal.

Dr. Price made his way to the front of the formation.

"Is he alone?" asked Price.

"There's more in the tree line," said Daniel.

"Has he—"

Before Price could finish his question, the tiny man stepped up to the doctor and put his right hand against Price's chest. Price returned the greeting solemnly. As if on cue, more natives stepped out on the path, ten in all, each carrying some kind of primitive weapon, none looking menacingly at the foreigners.

"What do they want, Price?" asked Cal.

"I don't know."

"Are they the same tribe?"

"Yeah. I recognize the leader. I'll bet they were out when the Colombians attacked."

The leader of the small band stepped around Price and moved amidst Cal's men, making his way to the middle of their hasty grouping. Everyone watched as the tiny man reached their captive and pointed a dirty finger at the squirming pirate.

"I think he wants him, boss," said Gaucho.

"No. No, please! Keep here!" said the prisoner, trying to back away but held in place by the immovable Trent.

"Let him go, Top," ordered Cal.

Trent nodded and released the man's restraints. Eyes wide, the man tried to flee. Quicker than Cal would've imagined, the tribal warrior made some clicking sound and two of his men sprinted after the Colombian, pouncing on the man's back and pinning him to the ground.

"Quick little dudes," admired Cal.

"Aren't we going to take him with us?" asked Dr. Price.

"I think these guys deserve to have him more than we do. Anyone have a problem with that?" Cal asked his men.

No one did.

"Let's go."

Daniel led the way as the dying screams of their former captive faded in the distance.

THE WHITE HOUSE

President Zimmer yawned into his hand and he tried to focus on yet another piece of proposed legislation. It had something to do with wetland preservation in the Everglades. He yawned again and set the report down.

Travis Haden stepped in the door just as the president was rising from behind his desk. The former SEAL was in PT gear and looked to have just finished his daily workout.

"You got a minute?" asked Travis.

"Sure. I was just wrapping up."

"I just got off the phone with Cal. They're on their way home."

"Everything go as planned?"

"Not really."

The president sighed. While he loved Cal Stokes like a brother, and trusted the Marine like few others, there always seemed to be some level of 'fun' associated with his missions.

"What happened?"

Travis filled him in on what Cal had found, including the men who'd been wounded.

"Is everyone going to be okay?" asked Zimmer.

"They're fine. Just a few scratches."

Zimmer knew that probably meant Cal's men had been shot. A scratch to his elite warriors was a major trauma event for the average citizen.

"Anything we can do?"

"I asked and he said they're fine. Apparently this Dr. Price is pretty good at patching people up," said Travis.

"Good. What else?"

Travis crossed his arms. "I just heard back from my sources."

"Cromwell?"

Travis nodded. "I couldn't get anything concrete, but the guys I talked to described the colonel kinda like a kid describes the boogey man. They say he's bad news."

The number of nefarious characters hiding in plain sight under the auspices of the United States government never ceased to amaze the young president.

"What's he into?"

"We know he's got ties to the NIH and the CDC. I've pulled his file and it looks like your normal run of the mill Army career. He's hit all the wickets."

"But you don't buy it," said Zimmer.

"It's too clean. His record shows some short deployments to Africa, but he's been with the NIH for a while."

"Did you tell Cal?"

"I did."

"And what does he want to do?"

"He's gonna have Neil do some digging and asked me to do the same. He says we might want to ask General McMillan for a favor." Marine General McMillan was the current chairman of the Joint Chiefs and a trusted advisor to the president. It didn't hurt that he admired Daniel Briggs for his past exploits and had offered his assistance should they ever need it.

"Good idea. Why don't you see if the general has time in his schedule tomorrow. You don't mind running over to the Pentagon?"

"It's not my favorite place, but I don't mind," said Travis.

"Great. Let me know what you find out."

CHARLOTTESVILLE, VIRGINIA

After making sure his wounded were being cared for, courtesy of Dr. Price, Cal sauntered down to the kitchen to make himself a much needed nightcap. Their trip back from Colombia had been uneventful, but it had given him time to think about what the hell was going on. Clearly someone had anticipated their trip, but how could they have known?

As he sipped his Famous Grouse over ice, Cal mulled over his options. Travis was getting help from Gen. McMillan and Neil was doing his thing, hacking into whatever databases he could in order to find out more information on Cromwell.

What worried Cal was that Cromwell couldn't be acting alone. He had to have backers. No matter how ruthless the guy might be, it was virtually impossible for a relatively lowly Army colonel to have that much power.

No. There was someone else pulling the strings. But who were they and what were they trying to do?

ALEXANDRIA, VIRGINIA

Col. Cromwell re-read the email he'd received from his Colombian contact. There'd been no contact with the group the cartel had sent to ambush any follow-on force. He should've had Malik Vespers stay there after searching the village.

But the former Secret Service agent was too valuable to Cromwell. Even now the mute was off on another errand, shoring up a vital part of Cromwell's plan.

He could feel the attack coming, had been in the business too long not to protect himself. Well, let them come. He'd take care of anyone who thought they could get in his way.

Cromwell closed his laptop and headed to bed, his conscience clear.

_____

HOBOKEN, NEW JERSEY

The security system reengaged as Malik Vespers completed the code on the keypad. The beep of the alarm echoed up into the rafters of the high ceilinged warehouse.

Another mission complete. His boss would be happy and that made Vespers happy.

The former Secret Service agent derived pleasure from serving his master, the man who'd saved his life years ago.

As a young agent assigned to the Secret Service's advanced party, he was tasked with ensuring the safety of an area that the president would soon visit. Vespers had excelled in his duties. Smart, capable and unwavering in his patriotism, the astute pupil was tagged as an up and comer, an agent who would soon be moved to the glamorous post on the president's personal security detail.

But that hadn't happened. After a particularly busy month on duty, Vespers and his team had arrived in Nigeria ahead of another stop in the president's world tour. Everything had gone according to plan until the night the agent in charge had given his men a much needed night off.

Normally not one to indulge in vices, Vespers accepted his colleagues' invitation to join them for a night on the town. They moved from bar to bar and soon found themselves in a high end brothel that served visiting dignitaries. The rest of the evening was a blur for the inebriated Vespers, but he'd woken up the next morning on the crude dirt floor of a prison cell.

Days passed and no one came for him. Not his team leader. Not his fellow agents.

On the fourth day, a gap-toothed hulk in faded utilities visited him. It was the first face he'd seen since being interred. The man had calmly explained in broken English that Vespers was now property of Mohammed Yusuf, the leader of the fledgling group of Islamic fanatics who would later be called Boko Haram.

The man told Vespers that he was being charged with crimes ranging from rape to overindulgence. Vespers pleaded with the man to get a hold of American authorities, but the requests were ignored.

After being beaten into submission, he was blindfolded and subjected to a ride in the back of a blacked out extended cab pickup truck. He didn't know it at the time, but Vespers soon found himself in the northeastern city of Maiduguri, the center of his captors' burgeoning empire.

He was brought before a gathering of elders, who swiftly condemned the American, the translator telling Vespers that he would be ritually mutilated then dismembered starting with his tongue. The translator calmly explained that his tongue would go first so that the foreigner could no longer spread his evil throughout the world.

They'd done it with a rusted blade heated over an open fire. The tip of his tongue held by a pair of pliers, his head strapped to a wooden post. Oh, how they'd howled with glee at his pain.

They left him tied to a wooden post, each passersby spitting on him and throwing stones. Kicks and hits with the butts of rifles. He'd prayed for death, once even trying to hang himself with the rope that held him to the post.

It hadn't been God who'd answered. It was a human avenging angel who'd come to his rescue.

Vespers would never forget the day he'd first seen Col. Cromwell, striding into the compound behind his raid force. They'd finally found him, and it was Cromwell, who'd been in the area on a relief mission, who had insisted on leading the rescue.

Cromwell had ordered his men to untie Vespers and had given him his own canteen to drink from. Vespers often thought of that moment, how the water had run over his swollen stump of a tongue, the cleansing coolness gifted by his savior.

"You're going to be okay, son," Cromwell had said.

And he was, for the most part.

Vespers contracted numerous afflictions due to his captivity and the fact that his captors made him eat his own feces as they stood back and laughed. Hepatitis. Giardia. But the most damaging effect was to contract a never-before-discovered strain of congenital analgia. In its most common form, the disease is typically discovered at birth and precludes the infected from feeling pain or even hot and cold. The majority of those with congenital analgia never live past their twenties. But while the traditional disease puts the afflicted at risk due to the inability to realize they're hurt, Vespers experienced a muted form.

Instead of not feeling pain, the sensation normally associated with pain was merely dulled. During his rehabilitation, he found he could push himself farther than before. Cromwell said he'd been given a gift, a new superpower. Vespers believed him.

So when the Secret Service terminated his employment and denied any sort of compensation due to the scandal he and his comrades had started in Nigeria (three others were forced to resign along with the advanced team leader), it was Col. Cromwell who'd been there for him. He'd offered him a job, citing a need for someone who knew the ins and outs of security.

Vespers didn't hesitate. He accepted on the spot. From that day on he was Cromwell's man. Much like the Luca Brasi character was to Don Corleone in *The Godfather*, Vespers became a pillar in Cromwell's empire. A loyal companion. A ruthless enforcer. An unquestioning sentinel at his master's side.

VESPERS SMILED as he got into his rented Toyota Camry. Another successful mission. His master would be happy.

WASHINGTON, D.C

8:27AM, APRIL 9TH

Senator Thompson's good mood was gone. He'd spent the previous night with his son. They'd begun with a movie and then moved on to dinner and drinks at one of Michael's favorite hangouts. Thompson had watched as his son kidded with friends and just looked...alive. He'd found it hard not to stop from crying, so great was his relief. If only his wife could have shared that moment with them.

But now everything was starting to unravel. Cromwell reported that Price had somehow made it down to Colombia with a team of unknown operatives and miraculously escaped the ambush. Cromwell's competence was waning in Thompson's eyes, but the senator had to be careful. The crafty colonel knew too much, had his fingers on too many strings.

Not that he, Senator Mac Thompson, would admit to it. *He* was the senator, *not* Cromwell.

Things had moved too fast after Price's discovery. There hadn't been time to insulate himself with the layers needed to escape possible culpability. He'd have to be careful. There had to be a way he could outmaneuver all sides and come out on top. It's what he did. It's what he'd always done.

He stared at the picture of him and his son on his desk. Luckily Michael would never have to know, would never have to make the same sacrifices his father had. At least he'd have a chance at a normal life. If all went to plan, their life would be set. Michael would never have to work. Sen. Thompson had even considered retiring from public office and traveling the world with his boy.

But deep down something told him that wouldn't happen. He loved the game too much. Thompson played politics just as he had baseball, with a great deal of skill and a smattering of self-induced luck. Well, at least he'd come out on top. He'd never won a World Series ring, but he was convinced that the White House was not out of the question.

———

Col. Cromwell marched into Sen. Thompson's office like he was on the parade deck, standing centered two feet from the front of the politician's desk.

"What do you have to say for yourself, Colonel?" asked Thompson, not looking up from his work.

"What would you like me to say, Senator?"

Cromwell wasn't going to give the senator an inch, but he would let him believe that he was the one with all the power. It's what all politicians wanted, to be the person controlling the rest of the room.

"How about you tell me why on God's green Earth we don't have Dr. Price in custody yet?"

"I won't give you excuses, Senator. You've heard everything we've done to find him. If that isn't enough, I'd be happy to submit my resignation."

Thompson looked up from his papers. Cromwell kept his eyes locked on the wall straight ahead.

"Would you cut that soldier bullshit. Sit down, dammit."

"Yes, sir."

Cromwell sat in one of the two leather armchairs facing the senator.

"Now, what are we going to tell our friends?" asked Thompson.

"All they need to know is that Dr. Price will soon be in custody and that the vaccine is contained."

"I assume you have a new plan to get Price?"

Cromwell nodded. "I do."

"Are you going to tell me what it is?"

Cromwell smiled. "You'll be hearing about it soon enough. Keep an eye on the news today, Senator."

———

EVERYONE, including the normally up-at-the-crack-of-dawn Daniel Briggs, had opted to sleep in. Dr. Price wandered down to the kitchen to find some coffee, nodding to the now familiar faces of Neil Patel and Jonas Layton, who were deep in discussion, probably about some tech innovation that was way over his head.

Two operators, Price couldn't remember their names, were watching CNN in the living room. The news anchor was talking about the latest string of violence in Iraq. *What a waste*, Price thought, remembering the friends he'd lost in the desert.

After sipping his coffee, Price moved to the fridge to find breakfast. His hand reached for the handle but stopped. He swiveled toward the television.

"Can you turn that up?" asked Price.

One of the guys did. Price moved closer, his appetite gone, legs weak.

Federal Investigators descended on the offices and warehouses of Price's Imports. The FBI has taken control of their headquarters in Hoboken, New Jersey as well as satellite offices in New York City, Los Angeles and New Orleans.

An FBI spokesman told us over the phone that the entire Price family, including those not directly involved in the conglomerate's operations, is now being investigated for links to terrorist organizations in Poland and Ukraine.

At this time we cannot confirm a report that says weapons grade biological components were found in one or more of the company warehouses. We'll update you as soon as we have more...

Price stared wide-eyed at the television screen. Terrorists? Biological weapons?

He put a hand out and braced himself against the wall for support. Everything was spinning. His entire family. Who had...

His eyes blazed with clarity. *Cromwell.*

"You okay, Doc?" asked one of the men sitting on the couch.

Price nodded. "Where's Cal?"

CAL DIDN'T RESPOND. Another wrinkle. Someone was getting smart, going on the attack instead of waiting for the other shoe to drop. Worst case, Cromwell knew or at least had some idea of who was helping Dr. Price. Best case, Cromwell was fishing. Cal might've played it the same way had he been on the other side. Rattle Price's nerves by going after his family.

It had worked. The already shaken Price was falling apart in front of the Marine. But now wasn't the time to panic.

"Look, I know how these things work. I've personally been through it before. Let us make a couple calls and the worst that'll happen is your family spends a little time in questioning. I assume they have the money for attorneys?"

Price nodded, his face a blank sheet of pain.

"Good," continued Cal, wanting to get Price out of his funk and back to work as soon as possible. He'd learned that lesson time after time in the Corps. Idle mulling wasn't good. Getting the affected back on task as soon as possible was. "Let's get everyone together and come up with a game plan. We'll need your help."

Again Price nodded, but didn't say anything.

CHARLOTTESVILLE, VIRGINIA

10:15AM, APRIL 9TH

The news wasn't good. Neil had confirmed that the FBI had, in fact, found biological components in Price's Imports's Hoboken warehouse. Worse still, they were starting to connect the dots. Not only were they looking at relationships with overseas suppliers, they were also dusting off Dr. Hunter Price's old file, the one marked *DECEASED*.

Suddenly Price was on the government's radar again and that wasn't good. Facial recognition technology had improved, as had other passive and overt investigative methods since 9/11. Due to the supposed terrorist connection, the government now had carte blanche. They could shut down Price's Imports indefinitely and keep the family tied up in investigations for years.

Cal's inner circle sat in the War Room batting around ideas, trying to come up with a course of action that could work. Unfortunately, Cromwell had them by the proverbial balls. If they took the risk of coming out of the shadows and then somehow got caught, their entire operation could be shut down before they could do any good. Cromwell had already proved to be a master strategist. The only thing he didn't have was Dr. Price.

"The way I see it, we need two things. First, we need to find out what the hell Cromwell is doing. What's his plan? Second, we need to get our hands on Cromwell," said Cal. "Neil, how close are you to getting into his system?"

Neil Patel adjusted his glasses, a sign that things weren't going according to his typical, exacting schedule. "They've got a lot of security surrounding whatever they're doing. I haven't seen this level of lockdown in a while. I can keep trying, but I think the best option is to somehow get someone inside."

No one liked that idea, least of all Cal. It was one thing to break into a remote facility miles from civilization. It was quite another to sneak into a government building in the middle of a densely populated city.

"Who's got an idea of how we can do that?" asked Cal.

"What if we did both?" asked MSgt Trent.

"You mean nab Cromwell *and* force him to tell us what's going on?"

"Yeah. It'd be easier to pick the guy up and have Doc Higgins use his magic juice," said Trent, throwing an appreciative nod Higgins's way.

For the first time since they'd gathered, Price spoke up. "That won't work. Cromwell not only has guys like Malik Vespers watching over him, but he's got passive alarms in place as well. The second he senses something's wrong, he'll push the panic button."

Cal didn't know how accurate Price's claim was, but he kept his thoughts to himself. By the looks of some of the others, they were thinking the same thing.

"Wait!" said Price. "I can't believe I didn't think of it before. There may be an easier way. I'm not supposed to know this, but a few years back Cromwell started outsourcing some of his research to private labs. I only found out because I happened to bump into an old buddy who'd gotten out of the Army and was running a lab up in Delaware. He's was in town to hand deliver data to Cromwell."

Cal perked up at the revelation. "Do you know where they're at?"

"Not exactly. But I assume there has to be some paper trail for the funding, right?"

"That's not always the case, but we'll see. Neil, why don't you start looking into it. Jonas, do you mind helping him?"

"No problem," said Jonas.

Cal nodded, his pulse quickening. He could feel the familiar tingle of the hunt. "Great. It's not much, but at least it's something."

AN HOUR LATER THEY RECONVENED. Neil stood in front of one of the large computer screens to show them what he'd found.

"Okay. I couldn't find a lot, but here it is. I was able to track the funding linked to Cromwell's office. Some of it's pretty thin, but I connected the dots thanks to Jonas's help and came up with a list of seven facilities that could be a match."

Jonas took over. "There were a lot more that we could've scrutinized, but based on the research, we figured these were a good bet. We were able to get the names of the lead researcher, the projects they've got funding for, and the location of each facility. I'm going to go down the list and I'd appreciate it if you'd tell me if anything sounds familiar, Dr. Price."

Price nodded.

"Okay," said Jonas. "The first facility is a small lab just

outside Myrtle Beach. The head of the research is a doctor by the name of..."

BY THE TIME Jonas had gotten through six of the seven labs, Price was more discouraged than before. Not one of the descriptions came anywhere near something that could be connected to his cancer research. To make matters worse, there's wasn't a name listed that he recognized. While that seemed strange given the limited size of the research world, it didn't surprise Price. Cromwell had been careful. No links. He was sure the seventh would be another dead end.

"The last of the seven is located on the outskirts of Fredericksburg, Virginia. The lead researcher's name is Marcel Merrifield."

The name didn't ring a bell. Price exhaled. Time was ticking and he could only imagine what his family was going through. He was sure his grandfather was rolling over in his grave.

Jonas continued. "Dr. Merrifield got a grant a couple months ago for something called molecular destabilization. It doesn't give any—"

"Hold on. Say that again," said Price, something in his subconscious firing from a long discarded memory.

"Which part?"

"What did you say they were studying?"

"Something about molecular destabilization and its origins within racial populations."

My God. The forgotten conversation came to Price like a crack of thunder. He'd been talking to one of his staff about an X-Men movie. The one where Magneto helps Jean Grey magnify her powers after bringing her over to the dark side. It had come up because of what they were doing with the substance the medicine man had given Price in Colombia. In essence, it was changing cancer on a molecular level, something akin to molecular manipulation. Instead of remaining in its original form, the cancer was being told to change, to morph into something else.

The two researchers hadn't even noticed Col. Cromwell until he'd asked a question about how it might work in reverse, like in the movie. Price had thought it an innocent enough question, more fantasy than reality, so he'd answered truthfully.

Someone's voice shook him from his thoughts. It was Cal.

"What is it, Doc?"

Price closed his eyes, replaying the conversation and matching the language with what Jonas had just read. Cold fear gripped him as he considered the implications.

"Doc, what are you thinking?" Cal asked, a bit impatiently.

Price's face had turned ashen, and he couldn't keep his hands from shaking.

"We had it all wrong," he said, just above a whisper.

"What?"

"Cromwell doesn't want the cure...he's developing a weapon."

BETHESDA, MARYLAND

11:39AM, APRIL 9TH

Col. Cromwell smiled as he read Dr. Merrifield's email. Things were finally starting to go his way. Not only were the Feds putting the squeeze on Dr. Price's family, his handpicked team in Fredericksburg was close to their objective.

Serum viable. Initial tests promising. Not as long-lasting as we'd hoped, but with a few minor adjustments, I foresee successful completion sooner than expected.

Cromwell liked Merrifield's style. The French-born researcher had the ability to piss off his colleagues, but Cromwell had pegged him right from the start. While most firms might consider Merrifield a maverick, reckless in his pursuits, Cromwell understood what the man wanted. Money and recognition.

Such ambitions were easily manipulated. Not only had he swooped in with funding just as Merrifield had once again been denied for another project, he'd also promised to give the scientist all the credit. To a man who'd been laughed at during dinner parties and talked about behind his back for years, Cromwell's offer was like the opening of Heaven's gate for Merrifield.

Cromwell had gone out of his way to make Merrifield feel important. He'd also given him more funding and independence than he'd ever had in his career. The project wasn't easy, but the French-American devoured the task eagerly. Just as the email had said, not only were they making progress (where others had failed), but they were also months ahead of schedule.

He fired off a quick congratulations and looked forward to seeing him soon. Cromwell ended the email by asking if there was anything else Dr. Merrifield needed, knowing that the snob would probably ask for an overnight getaway to Aspen to recharge or an escort for the night. It was a small price for Cromwell to pay and would keep Merrifield chugging along at his relentless pace.

Cromwell pressed SEND and sat back in his chair. Pretty soon he'd be able to tell everyone, even Senator Thompson, to fuck off because he would be untouchable.

————

CHARLOTTESVILLE, VIRGINIA

Dr. Price had explained to Cal's team what he imagined his old boss was doing with the research. It sounded like something out of a fantasy novel to Cal. To have the ability to manipulate a human body on the molecular level.

They had to get inside the research facility and see what they could find. Cal was waiting on a call back from the president with the go-ahead. The quicker they could pin something on Cromwell the better. Cal wondered how high the intrigue went, having experienced more than his share of government conspiracies since leaving the Marine Corps.

There were all kinds of ways politicians and their cronies could misspend taxpayer money. So far it looked like this project had been privately funded, but it still had to be linked to the American government if Cromwell and his office at the NIH were involved. Surely an Army colonel couldn't be the man sitting behind the curtain. No, there had to be one or more people hiding in the shadows.

THE WHITE HOUSE

President Zimmer didn't like what he saw. Another program that had somehow gone unnoticed by the previous administration. How many covert deals were being conducted without his knowledge?

Zimmer looked up from the file.

"Do we know who else is involved? I'm sure Cal will want to know."

Travis Haden shook his head. "That's all I could get without Cromwell getting a whiff of my snooping. I'm sure we can get more, but it might send them scattering."

"So you think we should let Cal try?"

"I think it's worth a shot. He knows what he's doing and he knows what's at stake."

The president leafed through Travis's notes. Any kind of biological weapons being developed on American soil, and under the auspices of an Army colonel no less, had the ability to cripple his administration. Anyone and everyone would assume that the president knew about it.

There were risks, but Zimmer agreed with Travis, it was

worth it. If Dr. Price's hunch was right, they needed to know what the research entailed.

"Call Cal and tell him to do it."

———

CHARLOTTESVILLE, VIRGINIA

"It's a go." Cal stood up from the conference table and stretched.

"When do we leave, boss?" asked Gaucho.

"Let's hit it tonight. We can plan on the way."

Gaucho nodded and moved to prep his team.

"Where do you want us?" asked Neil.

"I want you, Jonas, Price and Doc Higgins to hang here. I'm assuming that once we tap into their system we can shoot to you remotely, right?"

"No problem," said Neil.

Everyone knew their place. Cal didn't have to do any hand-holding. The warriors would take care of the infiltration and the brains would stay back and support. It was a scenario they'd played out countless times. Hopefully it would go off without a hitch.

———

FREDERICKSBURG, VIRGINIA

Dr. Marcel Merrifield examined the last batch of slides for the day. He'd been at it for hours. His assistants called him The Machine. Not one to take breaks or let up from his hectic schedule, Dr. Merrifield expected the same from his staff.

Since taking over the project, he'd carefully doled out

assignments, keeping information compartmentalized. Opposing sections weren't even allowed to socialize together. He was the only one who knew the breadth of what they were developing, and he kept his teams under constant watch. They knew they were working on something big, mostly because requests for funds or new equipment were almost always approved right away. The researchers didn't care what the final product was. They were worker bees used to carrying out orders, happy to get paid to do what they loved.

The handful of scientists who'd asked too many questions were quietly ushered to the door.

Merrifield couldn't sleep most nights, dreaming about the implications of his research. He'd had lofty goals before, but with the seed planted by Cromwell, Merrifield knew his detractors would soon have a change of heart. Much like the sequestered scientists at the Manhattan Project, Merrifield felt like he was on the verge of making history.

He'd show them all, and then he'd reap the rewards.

FREDERICKSBURG, VIRGINIA

1:49AM, APRIL 10TH

Their first option had worked. Rather than trying to sneak into a one-story building, somehow avoiding the front desk rent-a-cop, and accessing the sure to be highly secure labs, Neil had suggested they try something else.

"It might be possible to gain access from the outside. As long as you can get me into their wiring system, I can figure out the rest."

It hadn't been quite that easy, but almost. They were in the process of uploading the data to Neil when a small convoy pulled up to the front of the office building.

———

COL. CROMWELL KNEW the value of a surprise inspection. He'd learned it walking the defensive perimeter first in training as a second lieutenant, and then in real combat in remote locations around the world.

He'd given Merrifield a heads-up, but had told him not to

say a thing to his staff, a portion of which were on the night shift.

Dressed in a suit and tie, accompanied by Malik Vespers and his handpicked team of seven men, Cromwell strolled into the building.

———

"WE'VE GOT nine visitors up front. Seven went inside. Another two are headed around the building," said Trent over the radio.

"Shit," muttered Cal. The uplink wasn't done. "How much more time do you need, Neil?"

"Maybe two more minutes."

Cal looked at Daniel, who was similarly dressed in dark street clothes. "Plan B?" asked Daniel.

Cal and Daniel were the only ones exposed, hugging the edge of the brick building as best they could.

"Yeah, let's do it."

———

DEXTER JAKE AND HIS PARTNER, Paul Wyer, did a slow sweep around the office building. Cromwell had told them to do a quick once over. They weren't expecting to find anything, but an inspection was an inspection.

Dexter had worked for Cromwell, or more specifically for Malik Vespers, for just over two years. He didn't mind getting his hands dirty and the pay was pretty good. Besides, nobody fucked with them. Vespers saw to that and so did Cromwell. Dexter didn't miss his days on the police force. Boring duty. Endless patrols. Shit. He'd take a midnight inspection over a desk job any day.

They'd just rounded the back corner when he thought he

heard the sound of running water. "You hear that?" he whispered to his partner.

"Yeah. Probably one of the drains."

Dexter unholstered his pistol and flicked on the flashlight mounted below the muzzle. Wyer did the same.

They soon found the source of sound. Some guy and his buddy were pissing on the rear wall of the building. One of them raised a hand and shielded his eyes from the bright beams of the flashlights.

"Can't you see we're trying to take a leak," came the slurred voice.

Wyer chuckled.

"Finish up and move along," said Dexter.

The guy with the blond ponytail gave him a shit-eating grin and nodded, wavering a bit, shaking off the end of his piss.

Vespers' troops waited for the two men to zip up their flies and move on.

"Thanks for watching us piss," said the second guy, taking a swig from a small bottle of booze he'd pulled out of his pocket. The two drunks giggled at the joke, stumbling away from the building. Dexter rolled his eyes and kept walking.

"You think we should tell the colonel about that?" asked Wyer.

Dexter snorted and moved on.

———

ONCE THEY'D GOTTEN FAR ENOUGH AWAY from the complex, Cal and Daniel stopped their fake shuffle and joined up with the others.

"Did you get in?" asked Cal.

"Yeah. I'm in," said Neil.

"Good. We're getting out of here."

The extraction was otherwise uneventful. No alarms. All men accounted for. With the adrenaline wearing off, Cal dozed as they made the hour and thirty minute drive back to Charlottesville.

————

"EVERYTHING LOOKS GOOD HERE, Dr. Merrifield. Keep up the good work," said Col. Cromwell.

Merrifield tried to keep a straight face, but a smile peeked out. He was happy to please his benefactor.

"Is there anything else you'd like to see, Colonel?"

"I think we'll get out of your hair and let you get back to work."

"Thank you."

Merrifield walked his unofficial boss to the door and promised a significant update soon. He was so close and couldn't wait to share it. Still hours from sleep, Merrifield marched back to his private lab and got back to work.

————

CROMWELL WAS PLEASED. Merrifield ran a tight ship. Despite the late hour, the scientist looked to be at the top of his game. He was like a kid in a candy store, full of excitement despite his attempts to remain nonplussed.

They were nearing successful completion of a solution that would change the world. And to think those healthcare idiots thought it was all about them.

Cromwell dialed a number, knowing that the senator would be waiting.

"Yes, sir. We just finished. Everything looks good."

————

CHARLOTTESVILLE, VIRGINIA

Neil clicked one last key and sat back. His custom made programs would do the rest of the heavy lifting. Now that they had access, it was simply a matter of getting past the facility's security. That would take a few hours, but Neil wasn't worried. He'd done it too many times to count.

Rather than sit and watch, Neil gathered up his things and headed off to bed.

WASHINGTON, D.C

7:38AM, APRIL 10TH

Senator Mac Thompson rolled his eyes in response to the ongoing bickering on his computer screen. Two CEOs, including Waldo Erickson, the obese head of Hampstead Healthcare, were going back and forth about what to do with the cancer vaccine once it was in their hands. Erickson wanted to shelve it. The others wanted to develop a weaker vaccine and milk the profits for as long as they could.

It was the same tired conversation they'd had for months. Thompson didn't care. Their needs weren't his concern. He had to keep them happy because he needed their money.

But if they ever found out what their funds were really paying for...

Thompson wanted to laugh. The men and women on his screen thought they had all the power, but they didn't. He did. He'd played a passive role since the beginning, simply introducing the existence of the cure to the secret group. At first there'd been shock, mute disbelief. But then the tide turned just as Thompson knew it would.

A cure for cancer meant many things. It meant hope for terminally ill patients around the world. It meant the possible eradication of the number two killer. But it also meant a serious blow to the healthcare industry. There were trillions of dollars at stake.

What would oncologists do without cancer patients? What would pharmaceutical companies do without any demand for their cancer fighting drugs? What would non-profit cancer organizations do without a constituency to protect?

The shrouded collective Thompson now watched via video conference was made up of the leaders of those entities who would be most affected. He'd first approached the bombastic Waldo Erickson, who'd then gathered the rest. While they might be competitors in their day-to-day activities, this cure was a common enemy.

As time went by, and the search for Dr. Price dragged on, their fear had only grown. That fear enabled Thompson and Cromwell to funnel more and more money where they needed. So while the greedy bastards were trying to protect themselves, Thompson was building a solution.

There was a problem bigger than cancer, bigger than the national debt that was threatening the United States of America. It was an insidious plague that needed to be swatted back like a swarm of locusts. Sen. Thompson would soon have the weapon to do so.

He would never seek public recognition for what he'd done, but others would know. They'd suspect. They would see him as the man who'd come up with the answer.

The thought made the last thirty minutes of the conference call bearable.

———

MSGT TRENT WAS the first man in the War Room that morning. Normally an easy sleeper, he'd tossed and turned since getting home from their little jaunt to Fredericksburg. Like his friends, Trent had developed a sixth sense for things, often anticipating a situation before it happened. He was getting that feeling now, a premonition.

While he sipped his coffee, he scrolled through the day's headlines, not much catching his interest. He couldn't stand watching the news and preferred to soak it in at his own pace on the web.

A *DING* from the other side of the room caught his attention. It was Neil's computer. Curious, Trent got up and moved over to the computer screen that was flashing *SCAN COMPLETE.*

Neil's program had done its job hacking into the lab's database. Trent sat down and clicked the mouse, removing the alert. The screen was filled with file folders tagged by a wide array of names.

Trent didn't want to mess with Neil's stuff. Just as he went to get up and wake the genius, a bleary eyed Neil stepped into the room.

"I was just coming to get you," said Trent.

Neil tapped his cell. "I got the alert on my phone."

Trent pulled up another chair and watched Neil get to work. Even in his tired state, the techie clicked and scrolled faster than he ever would.

Neil mumbled to himself as he worked, getting into a rhythm as he methodically went through his analysis.

"What is all that stuff?" asked Trent.

"A lot of research. It looks like they've got different teams feeding their data to a central user. That's probably the Merrifield guy." A moment later he confirmed his statement with a grunt.

"How long is this gonna take?"

"I don't know. You'll have to ask Price. I'll just get it organized for him."

"I'll go wake him up. I'm sure he wants to feel useful. Poor guy's been moping around like a sad puppy dog."

PRICE WAS ALREADY AWAKE and followed Trent down to the War Room where Neil had almost finished whatever he was doing. He nodded to them as they entered but held up his index finger to get a minute more.

Trent settled in next to Neil while Price stayed standing, trying to make sense of what he was looking at. He was anxious to confirm his suspicions, hoping the previous day's guess was way off the mark.

"Okay. What we're looking at is a copy. I did a little reorganizing so that you could find your way around," said Neil, giving his seat to Price.

It took Price a minute to get his bearings. He clicked through different folders, nodding and reading as he went. All standard research jargon. Hypotheses. Findings. Informal notes. More findings. Subjects.

"Guys, this might take me a while. Would it be a huge imposition to ask for a strong cup of coffee and some breakfast?" asked Price.

Trent smiled. "Breakfast is my specialty, Doc."

THIRTY MINUTES LATER, Price was getting antsy. An hour more and he was sure he'd been mistaken. There was no evidence to substantiate what he'd told the group. Doubt crept in. Maybe he was wrong. Was he looking for something that wasn't there? Had he risked the welfare of Cal's team on a whim? If that was the case, what did he really have?

He shook off the depressive thoughts and closed his eyes.

What was he missing? Taking a deep breath, he told himself to keep it simple. He'd learned from the SEALs that getting through BUD/S was as much about mental toughness as it was physical stamina. He'd laughed when a master chief told him, "You can't think about graduation from day one, Doc. It's all about getting from one meal to the next, breakfast to lunch, lunch to dinner. If the guys do that, they have a much better shot at making it."

Price soon found out the beauty in its simplicity. It really was all about taking things one step at a time, not trying to do too much and worrying about factors too far out of your reach. As long as you kept your head down and plowed from one task to the next, you'd make it. This was especially true in times of duress and fatigue, much as he felt now.

Opening his eyes with a renewed sense of purpose, Price started from the beginning. One folder led to another. Step by step.

WASHINGTON, D.C

The meeting hadn't gone as planned. Thompson had promised Cromwell certain things and now it seemed that the senator was reneging. As he walked away from the Capitol Building, the silent shadow of Malik Vespers at his side, Cromwell mulled over his options.

He wanted a command again. He hadn't had one since being a captain. That's what he'd been promised. He wanted a star. Again, something he'd been promised for fulfilling his end of the bargain.

He was the one who'd done it all and that arrogant Thompson would reap the most tangible benefits.

The fact that they were skirting U.S. law didn't matter. They both believed that the ends justified the means. Despite President Nixon's 1969 ending of all offensive biological weapons production when he declared, "The United States shall renounce the use of lethal biological agents and weapons, and all other methods of biological warfare. The United States will confine its biological research to defensive measures such as immunization and safety measures," and the U.S. ratified Geneva Protocol and Biological Weapons Convention, there was still biological testing being done.

Cromwell had almost memorized a portion of the Biological Weapons Anti-Terrorism Act of 1989 that defined a biological agent as:

> *Any micro-organism, virus, infectious substance, or biological product that may be engineered as a result of biotechnology, or any naturally occurring or bioengineered component of any such microorganism, virus, infectious substance, or biological product, capable of causing death, disease, or other biological malfunction in a human, an animal, a plant, or another living organism; deterioration of food, water, equipment, supplies, or material of any kind...*

What they were doing was against the law, plain and simple. But Cromwell didn't care and neither did Thompson. Hell, wasn't it God who'd rained down pestilence and destruction on the enemies of His people?

That thought made Cromwell smile. Not for the first time he considered the fact that the outcome of what they would soon implement could be seen as an act of God. How fitting. As long as everyone kept their mouths shut, and certain holes were plugged, it would happen just as they'd planned. The best part was that it couldn't be tracked back to them.

But until it was done he needed more insurance. No one would believe Price if he ever showed his face again. The man was dead to the world and his family's name was in the gutter. Price wasn't the problem anymore. It was Cromwell's supposed allies that worried him. The loose tongued health-care CEOs and the high-and-mighty Senator Mac Thompson.

But he was a soldier, and a damned good one. He'd wage a war without taking prisoners.

CHARLOTTESVILLE, VIRGINIA

Price's persistence paid off. He'd pieced together the seemingly random mix of data. While doing so, he realized that Dr. Merrifield probably had some way of descrambling the jumble, or maybe his mind just worked that way.

Price had read every word carefully, cringing as he digested how they'd twisted his own work, yet marveling at the skill it took to do it. Merrifield was like a world class composer, picking and choosing as he went, flexible with his hypotheses, never getting stuck on one conclusion unless it had been confirmed.

As a chef has certain signature dishes, so Merrifield had his own style. Decidedly out of the box yet comfortable with the classics. Price had never seen such seamless integration. Cromwell had chosen well.

Another folder and another dozen files. Price told himself he'd do one more and then take a break. His vision was blurring from the strain.

"Huh."

Neil, the only other person in the War Room, turned his head. "You say something?"

"No. Just talking to myself."

Price squinted then zoomed in on the file. It was a newspaper clipping from some foreign press. Now he could make it out. It was in Arabic.

"Hey, Neil, can you read Arabic?"

"I dabble."

"Can you come take a look at this for me?"

Neil came over and zoomed the image in even more. He read the short article out loud. Neil had a firm grasp of the language and translated without hesitation. Price listened.

"Why do you think that's in there?" asked Price.

"Beats me."

Price clicked another file open. Two more scanned images popped up on the screen. He couldn't figure out what the connection was. Why would Merrifield be...

Dr. Price's face went pale and his hand froze over the mouse, the curser blinking slowly.

Neil turned. "What is it?"

It took Price a few seconds to find his voice. "This is worse than I thought."

————

WASHINGTON, D.C.

Sen. Thompson hung up the phone and gazed out his office window. He watched as cars eased by, the tired pace a constant in the nation's capital. Thompson wondered what those Americans would think if they knew they were driving by a man who would soon ensure their safety, possibly for all time.

He'd come to see himself as the savior America needed. With increased pressure from around the world, his country was desperate for help. It wanted an answer just like it had wanted the bomb that dropped on Hiroshima. So many Japanese lives lost, yet so many Americans saved from invading the Japanese homeland.

This was his Hiroshima and Nagasaki all rolled into one. The research Cromwell was overseeing was only in its infancy, the first phase the crudest and most lethal. Merrifield had promised more innovation after the first launch. Better tools. More insidious. Deathly quiet.

Thompson believed in sacrifice. He'd never served in the military, but he respected the men and women in uniform. In fact, it was because of their sacrifice that he'd set out on this path. The trick was to use it without being its mastermind, at least to the world. He'd probably be drawn and quartered should his involvement be made public, but that wouldn't happen. He, Cromwell and Merrifield were the only ones who knew.

Merrifield would keep his mouth shut for money and glory. Cromwell would do it because he was a good soldier, even if Thompson couldn't make him a general. The money would help.

Thompson didn't relish the destruction they were about to rain down, but it was all part of the plan. After all, could there be peace without a little bloodshed?

WASHINGTON, D.C

The Situation Room was eerily still. Cal, Dr. Price and Jonas waited for the president to say something. They'd driven up from Charlottesville in a convoy, the rest of Cal's team now waiting outside. They were ready should the president give an order, which more than likely he would.

"Are you sure?" asked the president.

"Yes, sir," said Dr. Price.

"You're actually telling me that somehow, a rogue Army colonel has developed a biological weapon right under our noses?"

"Yes, sir."

"Explain to me how it works, Doctor."

Price began. "In a nutshell, they've figured out how to reverse my cure and use it as sort of a cancer magnet, a magnifier. Instead of getting the cancer to assimilate with a human body, their serum actually triggers a chain reaction. Everyone has dormant pre-cancer cells living in them, and we don't fully know why some people's become activated and others' don't. Merrifield's discovery triggers the cancer cells and accelerates their growth, exponentially. It's like a series of explosions going off in your body. To make matters worse, they've also figured out how to target based on race."

"How the hell do they do that?" asked Zimmer.

"Merrifield's specialty is DNA mapping. He figured out a way to hone in on a specific DNA marker. He's started with race."

"So you're saying that the drug may not affect me, but it could affect someone of Asian descent."

"Yes, Mr. President. Now, it might not be the broader Asian race, that could be all of us seeing as how we're all related, but it would be a small subset that he's somehow parceled out of the larger gene pool."

"I'll take your word on that, but there still seems to be the issue that most biological weapons have: deployment. Is Cromwell planning on going around injecting people with this stuff?"

Dr. Price's face colored. "No, sir. I...it was actually part of my research that helped them. I initially made the vaccine to be taken orally like the Colombian tribe had done. Its potency was the same as if I'd given it to them intravenously."

Travis spoke up next. "That's all good if you can make people drink it, but other than contaminating a city's water supply, that type of deployment doesn't seem like that big of a risk."

Price looked at Cal, who nodded for him to continue.

"Actually, they could," said Price, his face grave. "If I didn't loath what he's done, I'd call Merrifield an otherworldly genius. In the time he's had to develop this solution, he's not only figured out how to make it smart by targeting a person's DNA, but he's also figured out how to make it proliferate. He's made it contagious."

"You've got to be kidding me," said the president.

"I saw the evidence, and you know I'm not a science whiz," said Cal. "This stuff is bad news. Dr. Price is right. If it weren't so illegal and so deadly, it would be genius. But you haven't even asked the most important question yet."

"And what's that?" asked the president.

"Ask us who they're targeting."

The president's eyes narrowed. "Who are they targeting?"

"Arabs."

———

COL. CROMWELL HAD a world map spread out on the corner table in his office. He'd been one of the few to foretell the rise of Islamic radicalism, easily predicting its spread through the Middle East and now seeping into poor third world countries. The atrocities of 9/11 gave it a face.

He could remember getting the news about the World Trade attack during a fact-finding mission to Nigeria. He'd never felt so far away from his home, and yet, he wasn't surprised.

Other countries understood the threat. They'd battled it for centuries. The Israelis, the Brits, hell even the French. America was the new kid on the block, its citizens still naive to much of the horrors the rest of the world faced. In America, if you were hungry, you could go to the government for a hand out. In America, if someone threatened you, you assumed the police could handle it.

Cromwell knew evil. He'd seen it all over the world. While he'd busied himself with battling unseen diseases, he always kept his eye on the horizon, waiting for the next terrorist strike. It was inevitable. The United States stepped on too many toes. Not that it shouldn't, but the lapse of strength shown by the last president left a void that terrorists were only too happy to fill.

Col. Cromwell believed in a strong America, one who could not only dole out humanitarian aid, as he had through the years, but could also crush those who sought to keep their fellow man under foot. The new breed of terrorists was the evil he secretly wished to destroy.

When the idea had come to blend his new specialties with his ultimate desire, Cromwell jumped at the chance. Not only had Price's discovery been miraculous, but through a bit of imagination, Cromwell was given the ability to fulfill his dream.

Some men dreamt of wealth and power. Others spent their days whoring and polluting their bodies with foreign substances. Cromwell wished for revenge.

He saw every action he'd taken in his pursuit as a necessary step in accomplishing his task. If the civilized world wanted to stamp out extremism, the way to do it wasn't one by one. The best way, the way that would strike fear in the hearts of even the most radical extremists, was through something so invisible and so deadly that the most devout of followers would have no option other than to question their faith.

Yes, their women and children would have to die, but that was the price Cromwell was willing to pay. Us or them. You could not negotiate with terrorists. You could only kill them.

His hand swept across the coated map and he imagined the disappearance of every Arab in the Middle East, and then the world. While at first repulsed, countries would soon repopulate those areas. Like the Earth healing from a deep scar, so would the civilized world. They would come to realize that evil breeds its own death.

He was so close to holding all the power, to making his enemies kneel and ask for forgiveness just for a chance to live. Cromwell would not give it. There would be no remorse, just as there would be no quarter given to his enemy. This was a fight to the death, and Col. Gormon Cromwell meant to pave the way with the bodies of his foes.

WASHINGTON, D.C

The alert went out quietly, the heads of Federal law enforcement agencies notified first. No names were given and the specific threat was never mentioned. That meant only one thing: the White House believed there was a very real chance of an insider attack, something catastrophic.

Cal had tried to dissuade the president from pressing the panic button, but he'd been overruled. There were too many things that could go wrong. What if Cromwell's weapon got out? What if they'd already shipped? What if, what if, what if...

Cal didn't like what ifs. He'd learned in the Marine Corps that you could 'What If' a plan to death, because everything changed when the battle was met. He had the ominous feeling that the same thing was about to happen. Cromwell was too smart. He'd probably put contingencies in place just in case he was discovered.

A scheme of this magnitude went beyond simple mone-tary gain. Cromwell had something to prove and Cal would bet his life that the Army colonel would gladly go down swinging.

They'd located Cromwell at his office and were waiting for confirmation from MSgt Trent, who was posing as an NIH investigator, that he was still there. If he was, the president had authorized a joint operation with the FBI to take Cromwell into custody. Four teams were waiting around the block for Trent's signal, Cal among them.

The call came a moment later over the radio.

"He's not here," said Trent

"Does anyone know where he went?" asked Cal.

"His secretary said he'd be out for the day. Early dinner and then a meeting."

It would've been too easy. Cal hoped Cromwell hadn't been tipped off. If he had, they'd just missed their chance.

———

MALIK VESPERS DROVE with practiced precision, weaving in and out of Beltway traffic, slowing, then speeding. Never too fast, always in control. Cromwell sat in the passenger seat of their third vehicle, seething.

He'd received the urgent call just as he was outlining the final phase to Vespers. It was Senator Thompson who'd alerted him of the danger.

"You need to disappear for a while," Thompson had said.

"What happened?"

"They're passing word down from on high about a new threat. The way they're talking, it has something to do with an insider. Are you sure no one's been watching you?"

"You can never be one hundred percent sure, but we've taken the appropriate precautions," Cromwell answered, not convinced that he was in any real danger. He wasn't a novice. "Why do you think this is linked to me?"

"Let's just say the words NIH and biological weapons were thrown around. I had to pull some teeth just to get that much."

That couldn't be a coincidence.

"Okay. I'll take off for a while. You know how to find me."

They'd left the office through the underground garage, in a vehicle normally used by interns. Small, nondescript, and thankfully with tinted windows, the GM knock-off made the perfect first getaway vehicle. If anyone was watching, they'd be looking for his personal car, or possibly the pickup truck Vespers drove.

He thought as Vespers drove. There was only one person who'd have to the nerve to out him: Hunter Price. But how had Price gotten the word out? It didn't matter. What mattered was protecting his project at all costs. Cromwell was more than willing to give his life as long as he could deploy his weapon first.

If only Merrifield could speed up the process. Luckily no one knew about the facility or what was going on inside. He and Dr. Merrifield were the only ones who knew how to make sense of the data being mined by the teams at the Fredericksburg facility.

Vespers was just getting off at the Seven Corners exit when Cromwell's phone dinged. A text.

Cromwell read the message and smiled. He'd just gotten his answer.

———

"PACK EVERYONE UP. We need to get down to Fredericksburg as quick as we can," said Cal over the operational radio.

"We've got the pilots warming the birds up, Mr. Stokes," said the FBI agent assigned to lead the Bureau's contingent.

The man had been told to give Cal and his men anything they needed.

"Good." Cal hoped Cromwell hadn't gotten too far ahead of them. If they lost Merrifield, the president was going to lock down the whole east coast. He hoped for a little bit of luck.

————

DR. MERRIFIELD HURRIED through his office, packing the few items he thought he'd need. Cromwell's message had been clear: GET OUT NOW.

Merrifield knew what that meant. Someone had found out about his research. Just like Cromwell, this project had become more than a job for the French-born scientist. Sometimes he lay awake at night dreaming of his drug's spindly tendrils reaching out into the world, repaying the people who'd not only attacked his new home, but had also infiltrated his native country to an alarming degree.

When he'd first started his work for Cromwell, Merrifield hadn't completely understood. Now he did. It would take evil to defeat evil. Why wait until another attack hit the West? Cromwell's ideals had latched on to Merrifield's psyche. Hand in hand they would deliver the solution to the world.

As luck would have it, the night before was when the answer had come. He'd rushed back to the lab to see if his dream-induced epiphany would work. It did, and in stunning fashion.

He took one last look at his office and headed for the exit.

FREDERICKSBURG, VIRGINIA

5:45PM, APRIL 10TH

Once again, MSgt Trent volunteered to go in first. Armed with a personality that could talk its way past the sternest gatekeeper, plus a signed inspection affidavit from the NIH, the huge Marine chatted with the guards just inside the front door.

"I'm sorry, sir, Dr. Merrifield just left."

"Did he say when he'd be back?" asked Trent.

"He didn't. I'd be happy to take your contact information, or you're more than welcome to wait."

Neither of the pistol toting rent-a-cops seemed like they were lying. Trent shrugged. "Not a big deal. I was just in the neighborhood and my boss wanted me to check in on his work."

"Would you like me to get Dr. Merrifield's assistant?"

"Don't worry about it. Would you mind giving me Dr. Merrifield's cell phone number? The one they gave me says it's no longer in service. I'll give him a call and schedule something for tomorrow. My fault for not calling ahead."

One of the guards asked to see Trent's identification again, which he provided. "Yes, sir. Let me write it down for you."

TRENT HEADED BACK to the vehicle where Cal and Daniel were waiting. They'd already heard everything from the mic Trent was wearing concealed in his American flag tie.

The first thing they did was relay Merrifield's cell phone number to their FBI counterparts and to Neil, who was in a command vehicle a couple blocks away. Maybe they'd get lucky.

———

CROMWELL COULDN'T BELIEVE how quickly things had gone from bad to worse. Not only had he gotten messages from multiple contacts within the FBI and Homeland Security, the guards at the Fredericksburg lab also reported the visit of a Mr. Charles Randall, an investigator from the NIH.

Cromwell would've heard if his own hierarchy was sending someone to one of his facilities. No one ever went around him. This was another agency trying to get their hands on Merrifield and his research.

Luckily he'd gotten confirmation from Merrifield that he was safely on his way to their rendezvous point, research in tow. It wouldn't be long. With the completed formula in hand, nothing could stop them now. The cycle was almost complete.

He ignored his cell phone. Another text from Sen. Thompson. Cromwell had a feeling that the wily senator was involved with the leak. Maybe he'd gotten cold feet. Maybe he thought it was time to have Cromwell removed. It didn't matter. Within hours he would be gone, and there was nothing anyone could do to stop it.

————

PLUM TREE ISLAND NATIONAL WILDLIFE REFUGE

Gillespie Dukes sat in the captain's chair of his brand new seventy-six foot Viking Convertible saltwater fishing boat. Its robin's egg blue hull bobbed gently in the surf just off the point of the national wildlife refuge. His son was down below prepping the small inflatable they'd use to pick up their customers from shore.

Dukes waved to a freight liner cruising down the center of the Chesapeake Bay, heading out to sea.

Since childhood, Gillespie Dukes had known almost nothing but the sea. Raised in nearby Yorktown, Virginia, he'd cruised the countless inlets and byways of Mobjack Bay, Pocomoke Sound and, of course, the mighty Potomac. First he'd gone along with his father, a crusty fisherman. He hadn't known until he turned sixteen that his father did very little fishing.

"How do you think I paid for that nice house we've got on the bay, son?" his father had asked.

"Crabs?"

His father had laughed. "Did I ever tell you the story of your great, great grandfather?"

Gillespie had rolled his eyes. He'd heard the story a thousand times. According to his father, most of their ancestors were the noble pirates, or privateers, who'd worked the American coastline since before the United State's revolution. First employed by the lords of Great Britain, and then by rich colonists and revolutionaries, the Dukes had supposedly been into all sorts of smuggling and thievery. But Gillespie had always thought his father was pulling his leg, trying to get him to believe a truth stretched to impress a son.

"Sure, dad. You've told me a bunch of stories."

His father nodded, recognizing the look of bored disbelief in his son's eyes. "So you don't believe the stories?"

Gillespie shook his head.

"That's your right. Tell you what. Come with me tonight and I'll prove it to you."

Sixteen-year-old Gillespie had wanted to say no, to take off and meet up with his buddies in a little cove they'd found and drink the beers his friend Billy had snatched from his grandfather's fridge. But he knew his dad wasn't going to let up. Truth be told, he was a little bit curious.

Oh, how Gillespie's eyes had gone wide that night. Not a mile from where he now sat in his own boat, his father's old skiff met a boat full of Asians. Brought in by some container ship from China, the filthy stinking specimens were to be shuttled to their next destination. It was his father's job to get them there.

After the passengers were stowed and half the money paid, Gillespie sat on deck with his father's shotgun, told to make sure none of their cargo escaped. He often wondered if he could have shot someone at such a young age. Now he wouldn't think twice, but that had been his very first mission.

There'd been countless others over the years. Sometimes slaves. Other times weapons, exotic animals or counterfeit cash. He never really cared what he was delivering, just that he was paid. Once his father retired, he changed the business plan and always insisted on the full fee upfront. He was good for it and anyone who hired him knew it.

The job he was waiting to do now was his biggest payday in years, and might turn out to be his easiest. Three passengers and a leisurely trip out to sea. A piece of cake.

Everyone always enjoyed a first class experience when they hired Gillespie Dukes. This time more than others, thanks to his shiny new boat, courtesy of the hefty sum from his latest customer.

WASHINGTON, D.C

6:28PM, APRIL 10TH

Senator Mac Thompson paced back and forth across the Oriental rug. If he did much more of it he was sure to wear a path right down the middle.

His plans of getting away unscathed seemed fleeting. Not only was Cromwell not answering his calls and texts, he couldn't get anything from his contacts. The information chain had effectively been cut off. It was like flying in the dark, something the seasoned senator hated doing.

It reminded him of being a second stringer on his high school baseball team, a bench-warmer. Never in the know. Never the one calling the shots. Luckily, the summer after his freshman year Mac Thompson hit his growth spurt. Three inches taller, twenty pounds heavier, and his skills honed from hours in the gym and at the batting cage, sophomore first-baseman Mac Thompson throttled the returning senior for the starting job. He'd never looked back.

Now he felt like that scrawny freshman again, limited, powerless, in the dark.

He tried texting Cromwell once more, but there was no response. Maybe the soldier was just doing what he'd been told, lying low, being careful. Thompson wasn't worried about Cromwell being found, but he was worried about Merrifield's research and the implications should it get tied back to him. He couldn't let that happen.

The phone buzzed in his hand and he almost dropped it in surprise. It was Cromwell.

"Where have you been?" asked Thompson.

"Doing what you told me."

"Where are you?"

"I can't tell you that."

"Why not?"

"I'm not sure I trust you anymore, Senator," came the slow reply.

"What are you talking about?"

"I've had time to think."

"And what's that supposed to mean?"

"I find it convenient that you just happened to know about the authorities coming after me."

Thompson shook his head, trying to make sense of Cromwell's accusation. "I'm the one that called you!"

"Again, very convenient."

"What are you getting at, Colonel?" It was said in a tone that usually would have put the junior man in his place. It did not.

"I think it's time to say goodbye now, senator."

"Wait. What are you—"

"Say goodbye to your father, Michael," Thompson heard Cromwell say. He froze.

"Dad?" came Michael's voice over the phone.

Thompson wanted to scream. "Son, are you—"

"Your son's fine...for now," said Cromwell, once again back on the line. "Now here's what I want. You will—"

"You let my son go, you son of a bitch!"

"Now, now, Senator. I'd suggest you listen up if you want to have a chance of getting young Michael home safe and sound."

Thompson's heart felt like it was going to give out. He stumbled and only kept from falling to his knees by holding on to the end of his desk. He couldn't lose his son again. It was the only thing he had left that he gave a damn about. This time when he spoke it was as a broken man, resigned to his fate. "What do you want me to do?"

"Two things. First, I want you to call off the hounds. I don't care how you do it, just get it done."

"But I—"

"Second, you will meet me at a place of my choosing. Get yourself to the nearest helicopter pad and rent one for the night. I'll let you know where you can pick your son up, *if* you get the Feds off my back."

Thompson closed his eyes. "Is that all?"

"One more thing, and this is just an FYI. Our vision, our dream, is about to become a reality."

The line went dead and Thompson stared out the window into the darkening sky, an omen. He didn't know what he could do to call off the investigation. He didn't have that kind of clout. Nobody did.

But he had to try. He had to save Michael.

As he reached for the phone on his desk, his hand paused. Another option reluctantly crept into his mind. Gradually the idea took hold even as he tried to keep it at bay. He now had two options. Which to choose?

He picked up the phone and dialed the senate operator.

FREDERICKSBURG, VIRGINIA

7:04PM, APRIL 10TH

The FBI and Neil had both drawn up blanks. Dr. Merrifield's cell phone had either been discarded or destroyed. Neil's attempts at tracking it through the service provider came up with zilch. No pings.

Every other method they had at their disposal, including the combined databases of the CIA, Homeland Security and NSA, hadn't turned up a thing they could use.

Cromwell and Merrifield disappeared and had taken all the data with them. Neil confirmed the system scrub at the research facility. Everything of consequence was gone. They had the original copy, but without the final piece they had nothing.

"What else do we have?" Cal asked his team of operators. They'd been at it for what seemed like hours.

"What about Merrifield's family?" asked Gaucho. "Is there a way we can use them?"

"I already checked," answered Neil. "His parents died

years ago. No living relatives of any consequence, and the distant ones live overseas."

"What about Cromwell's superiors at the NIH?" asked Daniel.

"Travis said they were all clueless. Apparently the good colonel was something of an anomaly, given the ability to work autonomously without their approval," said Cal.

"And the CDC?" asked Daniel.

"Same thing. This guy's a fixer. You have a problem, you called Cromwell. Trav says he's got quite the reputation."

Cal looked to MSgt Trent. "What about you, Top?"

Trent shrugged his massive shoulders. "I'm stumped on this one. I know it's a long shot, but what about the mute. What's his name, Magic—"

"Malik Vespers," offered Dr. Price, whose eyes hadn't left the computer screen containing the files they'd copied from Merrifield's server. "Even if you get anything on the guy, I don't think it matters. He's a guard dog. All he cares about is what Cromwell says. Even if he had a wife and you threatened her life, Vespers probably wouldn't care."

That didn't leave anyone else. Once again Cal couldn't imagine how Cromwell had done it all by himself. How was that possible?

His thoughts were interrupted by his cell phone. It was Travis.

"What's up, Trav?"

Everyone waited as Cal listened to his cousin, his eyes narrowing. Trent and Gaucho looked at each other, concern clearly etched on their faces.

"You're sure?" said Cal. He couldn't believe what he was hearing. "Ok. We'll be there in ten minutes."

Cal replaced the phone in his pocket and looked up at his friends. "Looks like we may have a break in the case."

Sen. Thompson didn't have a choice. It was either this or let Cromwell have his son.

"We'll be there in five minutes, senator," announced the helicopter pilot.

Thompson nodded, looking out the window at the last glimmer of tangerine sunlight on the horizon. Not for the first time that night, he said a prayer for Michael's safe return.

I am now paying for my sins.

PLUM TREE ISLAND NATIONAL WILDLIFE REFUGE

The helicopter touched down, sending a swirl of blasting air through the marshy reeds. Gillespie Dukes covered his eyes with his hand and the bill of his well worn Tidewater Tides baseball cap.

Landing in the spot he'd marked with four chem lights minutes earlier, the helicopter's doors opened and expelled the last of the passengers. This one was a last minute addition, which meant a larger fee for Dukes. He was already counting the money in his head.

The figure climbed out, bag slung over one shoulder, dimly illuminated by the helicopter's interior lighting. Dukes could tell it was a man by his stiff gait. He moved out from his hiding spot just as the helicopter powered back up into the sky and clicked his flashlight on two times, getting the man's attention.

Once they were together, Dukes said, "Follow me. The dinghy's over this way. Stay close, though. The Air Force used to use this place as a bombing and gunnery range. All kinds of unexploded ordnance."

Dukes had only seen one piece of ordnance in all his years of traipsing through the wildlife refuge, and that had been a .50cal casing when he was a kid. The warning was a thing he liked to tell people to keep them in line. No sense letting his customers wander off without him. Hell, in two days he'd be putting a hefty down payment on another boat, one that his eighteen-year-old son could pilot and help expand their little empire.

He ran through his purchase options as they faded into the refuge, the sounds of the night escorting them to their transport.

———

COL. GORMON CROMWELL watched the approaching inflatable raft through his night vision goggles. Soon they'd be lifting anchor and heading out to sea. From what he'd seen of the boat's owner and his son, they knew their business and could probably be trusted to keep their mouths shut. He'd come highly recommended from a weapons merchant Cromwell knew.

They hadn't said a thing when Vespers threw the senator's son onboard or when Cromwell requested space for one more. He knew Dukes would gladly take the added payment for a little more time and one more trip to shore.

Dukes's son threw a line to his father and the rubber raft nestled in next to the larger craft. The captain was the first aboard and helped his final passenger up the ladder.

Cromwell moved to meet him after he'd stepped on the teak deck, an unsure look on his face. The soldier extended his hand in greeting. "Good evening, Dr. Merrifield. Are you ready to change the world?"

FREDERICKSBURG, VIRGINIA

S en. Thompson felt like he was going to have a panic attack. After calling the president to confess his sins and telling him about Michael's kidnapping, he'd been whisked away in an FBI helicopter bound for who knew where.

They'd met him in an unused little league baseball field, grass overgrown and now covering the old diamond. Fitting for the former baseball player.

The man who'd met him looked like a kid, a bit older than his son.

"Right this way, Senator," the boy with the rifle had said. He didn't bother offering his name and the senator didn't figure he had to introduce himself. He knew his place.

He was led to the old dugout and told to have a seat. There were more men waiting. They looked at him with barely disguised contempt. In their minds he was the enemy just as much as Cromwell. The men, all former military by their appearance, including one enormous black man, gathered around and took a knee as his escort spoke.

"Thanks to what the senator told the president, we've got a location on Cromwell. It looks like he's headed out to sea, but it doesn't look like they're in any hurry."

Sen. Thompson saw that the rest of the warriors deferred to this good looking young man. He was the leader.

"Do you know if my son's okay?" Thompson dared to ask.

The young man turned and gave him a leveled glare. "We're working on getting a drone on station as we speak." That was all the answer he got.

Instead of addressing him, the youthful leader went back to briefing his men. His tone was precise and his orders exact. No one argued against him.

"Are there any questions?" he asked.

Another man, a short Latino with a double braided beard, raised his hand, "What are our ROEs, boss?"

Thompson listened carefully, knowing that whatever rules of engagement they followed would affect the life of his son.

"We take them into custody if at all possible, but the main goal is to stop that virus from getting out of the country. If there's nothing else, let's get rolling."

They all stood and Thompson followed. Once again the young man escorted him away, accompanied this time by a stern faced man with a blond ponytail, his eyes reminding the senator of the penetrating look of a snake. The man with snake eyes carried a weapon Thompson knew to be a Marine sniper rifle. He couldn't remember what it was called, but he'd seen it put to good use in a couple of those dog-and-pony shows the Marines sometimes put on for visiting VIPs.

If the man was a Marine, maybe he had a chance.

"Will you save my son?" Thompson asked, his words coming out hoarse.

The young man looked back him and said, "We'll do our best."

———

THEY WERE RIGHT ON TIME. Cromwell had been in communication with their next transport that was loitering along the continental shelf far out into the Atlantic. There had been some traffic as they'd left the confines of the Chesapeake Bay, but it had thinned as they moved farther out to sea.

Luckily the ocean was relatively calm and Gillespie Dukes knew how to make a comfortable run.

He'd discussed the revised plan with Vespers and Dr. Merrifield. The most important thing was to get out of U.S. waters undetected. In a smaller boat that was possible. There was always the likelihood of being tracked from afar, but the boat they were on was one of thousands along the coast. If they were stopped, Dukes had all the paperwork to say they were on a deep sea fishing trip. They'd even gone so far as to change into civilian attire, floppy hats and all.

Cromwell had yet to hear from Sen. Thompson, but he didn't really care. He'd wanted to give the senator a shred of hope, but he knew what a long shot it was for the Thompson to actually stop the behemoth that was a federal investigation.

More than likely they would figure out that the senator was involved. And if they didn't on their own, Cromwell had some juicy evidence that would surely send Thompson's supporters scurrying and the Federal agencies slathering.

For the first time in days, Cromwell allowed himself to relax, sipping on a glass of Johnny Walker Blue that Dukes had offered as a thank you gift. Cromwell smiled as he wondered if Dukes had any clue what he was shuttling. No. Never in a thousand years would the smuggler think that he had the deaths of millions of people on his boat.

———

CAL WONDERED if the senator was going to puke. Thanks to the FBI's Hostage Rescue Team (HRT), who'd also provided a squad of their maritime specialists, they'd boarded three Sikorsky UH-60M Black Hawks. One held Cal's strike team. The second carried the HRT guys. The third flew with Neil, Dr. Price and some of the FBI's field geeks.

It was understood that Cal's team would go in first. The plan was to fast rope in and take down the vessel. There were a hundred things that could go wrong, but Cal had faith in his men. They were all experienced in this kind of thing.

In contrast to the pale senator, his men were ready. Steel eyed and all business. There was a time to joke and there was a time to strike. This was the latter.

As they closed in on their prey, Cal wished they'd gotten those drones he'd asked for.

ATLANTIC OCEAN

"Sir, you better get up here," Dukes called over the boat's intercom.

Cromwell stood from the leather swivel chair he'd been napping in, and headed above deck.

He found Dukes in the pilothouse talking with his son.

"What is it?" asked Cromwell.

Dukes pointed at one of three radars on his dash. This one, Cromwell knew, had the capability to track aircraft. Not a typical upgrade on a fishing boat, but a huge asset for a smuggler like Dukes.

"We've got three aircraft coming in behind us."

Cromwell came closer so he could see. Sure enough, there were three green dots closing the gap.

"What do you want me to do?" asked Dukes.

Cromwell didn't think it was mere coincidence that three aircraft, likely helicopters if he had to guess, could be making a beeline straight to them. But he didn't want to alarm his host.

"Just keep going. If they're coming after us, we'll deal with it in time."

"But we're still a ways from our rendezvous," said Dukes.

Cromwell stared at the man for a moment. "I said I'll take care of it."

Without waiting for Dukes's response, Cromwell left the wheelhouse and went to find Vespers. As usual, he wasn't far.

"We've got three aircraft, probably helos, headed our way. Get ready."

Vespers nodded and moved off.

Cromwell stepped to the side of the boat, ocean spray grazing his face as he looked back the way they'd been. He couldn't see them yet and that meant they had time. As was his way, Cromwell would be ready.

————

"TWO MINUTES," announced one of the Black Hawk crew members.

The fast ropes were ready to be thrown and his team waited in the order they'd decided to go in. Daniel, while usually the first to go, stood near the door with his trusty M40 sniper rifle. While he wished he could have his friend at his side, Cal knew the value of expert overwatch. If Daniel saw it, he could shoot it.

Cal tried to steady his breathing, but his heart still thumped in a steady rhythm. Anyone who said they weren't afraid before going into combat was an idiot. The trick was having the balls to do it.

This would be a first for Cal. He'd never done a takedown at sea. For that reason, Gaucho would be the first one out since he had the most experience while being part of the Delta teams. MSgt Trent would go next (the two had become inseparable), then Cal, then the rest of the guys.

"One minute."

Cal patted Trent on the back and threw a nod at Daniel, who was easing his rifle barrel out as one of the crew slipped open the door, blasting them with cold sea air. Sen. Thompson shielded his face and looked on, his eyes wide.

"Thirty seconds!"

Suddenly, alarms started going off through the helicopter. Cal's stomach clenched both as the helicopter banked left and he realized what had caused the sound. Anti-aircraft missiles.

The pitch of the aircraft threw the team against the bulkhead, jarring Cal in the process as his elbow smashed painfully against a fire extinguisher. Through the corner of his eye he saw something streak by the open door. It only took him a split second to figure it out. It was a missile that had narrowly missed them.

"Fuck!" he heard the pilot scream.

The bird flipped around again, somehow avoiding the incoming projectiles, but once again throwing Cal and his men like rag dolls back the other way. As his face rested against a window on the opposite side, he caught a flash, and then watched as the second helicopter caught another missile in its side and exploded.

"Shit."

They'd flown right into Cromwell's trap.

————

CROMWELL PATTED the younger Dukes on the back as he fired. The kid was well trained. While the first helicopter had gotten lucky and was now putting as much space between it and the boat, the second hadn't. Two missiles blew the thing out of the sky, making the third aircraft juke and follow its remaining companion.

"Bring the boat around and see if they want to try again," Cromwell ordered.

Dukes did as he was told, and turned the wheel, crashing them through their own wake.

Cromwell moved to join his companions and prepare for a possible boarding when he heard a strange sound from behind. He turned back and watched as the lifeless, and partially headless, body of the captain's son crumpled to the deck. In the next second multiple rounds hit the soviet era anti-aircraft mount Dukes said he'd kept as payment after a deal gone wrong.

Realizing the danger just in time, Cromwell dove behind a short wall as the missile mount exploded, taking a good chunk of the boat's hull with it.

He'd been lucky. Vespers crawled over to see if he was okay.

"I'm fine," Cromwell said. "Get ready for company."

———

CAL WISHED he hadn't brought the senator along, but got some satisfaction that the asshole was puking all over himself. Fuck him.

"Tell the other bird to stay away. We'll take it from here," he told the pilot.

"You still want to go in? Why don't we blow that fucker out the water?" asked the pilot.

"We need to get on the boat."

The pilot shook his head but didn't argue.

Cal turned back to his team. "Everyone ready for round two?"

ATLANTIC OCEAN

After making a wide turn, the Black Hawk came in just above the waves, the pilot hoping the low flight might muddle any radar on the boat. A slim chance, but a chance nonetheless.

"One minute," came the call.

It felt like everyone was holding their collective breath. Cal willed himself to take in slow lungfuls of air. That last pass had been a bitch. Luckily, Daniel said he was sure he'd taken out whatever jury-rigged anti aircraft mount on the side of the boat. He'd seen the thing explode.

"Thirty seconds!"

The helicopter flared up, trying to entice another round of missiles, but none came. Daniel was giving a thumbs-up from the doorway. Cal couldn't see a thing from where he was standing, but he trusted his friends. They were lined and ready, coming down to where they'd fast-rope in.

As they made their descent, Cal heard a muffled sound just as Daniel threw himself away from the doorway. A moment later flames licked in through the opening as a shock wave knocked the helicopter sideways, the aircraft yawing left harder than the last time, heading toward the waves.

————

CROMWELL WAS LED down the chrome-lined passageway by a porter wearing a ridiculous white sailor's outfit with crimson tassels and a matching bow tie that reminded the soldier of something he'd seen in a cartoon. They'd secured the senator's son, and Gillespie Dukes was hitting the rest of the bottle of Johnny Walker in memory of his son in one of the spacious cabins.

Entering the bridge, Cromwell marveled at the submarine's state of the art control room. He'd read about the Phoenix 1000, but he'd never set foot in one. With an overall length of around 213 feet, its beam 26-feet wide, the luxury submarine was built for the rich with lavish appointments custom crafted for whatever billionaire chose to build one. There were said to be less than a handful in existence.

Cromwell pushed past his guide and approached the man whose vessel had just saved them from imminent capture. It hadn't been how they'd planned it, but the timing worked out. With a little bit of luck, whoever had chased them down in their Black Hawks was now calling in the divers to find their bodies. All they'd find was the sunken vessel.

His host swiveled the oversized chair around, not without effort. His morbidly obese body practically oozed through the gaps between the chair rail and cascaded over the top.

"So good of you to join us, Colonel," said Waldo Erickson, CEO of Hampstead Healthcare, the owner of the underwater yacht.

"Thank you for helping with our getaway, Mr. Erickson," answered Cromwell with a smile.

The two were unlikely allies to the casual observer, but one need only look to the heart of the men to find their true motives.

"I hope that explosion didn't harm any part of my baby's hull. I'd hate to have to bill you for the damage." Erickson always sounded like he had food in his mouth. Probably because most times he did.

"I'm sure my benefactor would be happy to pay."

The two men smiled at each other and laughed. While at first they'd started out as bitter rivals, a little digging by Cromwell had found out a key piece of Erickson's past that few people knew.

On October 23, 1983, Erickson's brother, Marine Major Carl Erickson, was killed in the Beirut bombing by the Islamic Jihad. That alone was enough to make a man hate the Middle East.

To make matters worse, not a decade later, Erickson's other brother, James Erickson, had been murdered on August 3, 1990 during Iraq's invasion of Kuwait. The elder Erickson had been CEO of a Kuwaiti-based oil company.

Erickson's hatred ran deeper than even Cromwell's. It was simply a matter of putting hope into the man's fat hands and letting him do the rest. Whatever Cromwell needed, Erickson provided.

So while they argued and clashed in front of the others on conference calls, and accused the other of trying to derail the group's plans, behind the scenes they'd orchestrated the perfect scheme.

With Erickson's billions and Merrifield's formula, they would exact their revenge.

"Settle in for the ride, Colonel. Pretty soon we'll be toasting our victory."

THE WHITE HOUSE

8:20AM, APRIL 11TH

The president had just returned from his meeting with the director of the FBI. He'd offered his condolences for the men lost, and offered to give any public support needed. The director appreciated the sympathy, and told the president he'd be in touch.

Cal waited for Zimmer to take off his coat before saying anything. "They're sending a team down to the wreckage. We should have confirmation by noon."

Zimmer looked to his friend. "Tell me the truth, could the deaths of those HRT guys have been prevented?"

Cal frowned. "I don't think so. The Black Hawks were the quickest way to get us out there, and the missiles took us by surprise. I wouldn't even be here right now if it weren't for our pilot. Hell, he was probably just a split second quicker than the second pilot."

Zimmer nodded. "So what now?"

"Well, Cromwell did a pretty thorough job of destroying all of Dr. Price's work. Without the good doctor knowing, he'd already found the research and mangled it to the point that it's useless. Price has to start over."

"What does Dr. Price have to say about it?"

Cal shrugged. "I think he's just happy to be getting his life back. With Senator Thompson in custody and the Feds off of the Price family's back, maybe he can go back to living a normal life. I mean, he will have to go back to Colombia and find whatever substance he needs, but I don't think that bothers him."

"Please tell him that I'll do everything I can to help. Funding, material, you name it. This cure is much bigger than anything we've developed in our lifetime. With the senator's co-conspirators out of the way, maybe we can get back to actually fixing our healthcare system," said Zimmer.

"What did the others say? Why did they go along with Cromwell's plan?"

"They tried to clam up at first, throwing their lawyers at us, but we bulled past them. Once they found out what Cromwell was really up to, they haven't stopped talking. For them it was all about money. A cure for cancer meant no cancer treatments, meds, et cetera. They were going to lose trillions."

"I hope you lock those assholes up and throw away the key," said Cal, the thought of inhumane greed made him want to strangle every one of them. Not wanting people's lives to be saved all for money...

"I don't know how many of them will do time, but they will lose their positions and be publicly humiliated if I have anything to say about it."

Now that Cal thought about it, teaching a public lesson was probably better anyway. At least it might deter others from doing the same. He could live with that.

"What about Thompson? What's gonna happen to him?" asked Cal.

"I wouldn't be surprised if the guy had a heart attack. They had to sedate him earlier. Apparently the thought of killing millions couldn't do it, but the loss of his son sent him reeling. We'll see what happens."

While Cal could on some level understand the motives, killing a whole race with a superbug felt like cheating. He'd rather look into a terrorist's eyes as he blew his brains out than watch as countless innocents perished.

The door to the Oval Office opened and Travis stepped in, followed by Neil Patel, who was carrying an open laptop.

"I'm sorry for barging in, but you need to see this," said Travis, moving around the couch to give Neil room to set his laptop on the coffee table.

"What's going on?" asked Zimmer, trying to make out what was on the computer screen.

Clacking away like he always did, Neil didn't look up as he said, "This thing with Cromwell isn't over."

ISCHIA, ITALY

Gormon Cromwell, now going by the name Tom Hastings, walked along the cobblestone pathway that led to the villa he'd rented two days before. If all went according to plan, he'd decide to make an offer on the place, the view of the Gulf of Naples soothing his terminally antsy soul. Plus, the location on the side of the rock cliff gave them added security. It was perfect.

He'd just left the multi-million dollar laboratory Waldo Erickson had built earlier that year, just in case they needed an overseas back up plan. It had been Cromwell's idea, but Erickson had chosen the spot. He said he loved the thermal spas on the volcanic island and the expansive views from his palatial villa.

Merrifield was close to having the final product ready for shipment. Erickson had made a deal with a water exporter who would be shipping the contaminated bottles to select cities in the Middle East. To Cromwell's surprise, the Italian company even shipped to the heart of Satan himself, Tehran, Iran.

Cromwell felt like a teenager again. Not only were they close to their goal, he was also getting the free time he hadn't had since he was a kid. There was plenty of time to develop follow-on drugs, but meanwhile, he would enjoy the billions that Erickson was now sharing with him.

He knew there would soon be much more as the dying world paid any sum for the newly developed (it was already finished) vaccine that would save them from the cancerous superbug sweeping the world.

Cromwell strolled along happily, thinking that he might have to join Erickson at the fat man's favorite volcanic bath.

————

MALIK VESPERS WASN'T USED to not working. Now that they'd left the States, there wasn't much need for his services. He knew he'd always be taken care of, but he worried that he'd soon be bored.

Pushing himself out of the heated pool, the cool breeze followed him as he picked up his towel. He wrapped it around himself then turned to head back into the villa. *Shit*, he thought. He'd already forgotten his weapon. One week and he was going soft.

When he swiveled back to the chair where he'd left his Berretta, he was surprised to find a towering black man sitting there, casually twirling the pistol on the pinky finger of his left hand, another pistol in his right aimed at Vespers.

"What's wrong? Cat got your tongue?" asked the man.

Vespers growled.

"Oops. I forgot, you don't have a tongue, do you?"

The large man rose from his chair, still twirling, still aiming.

"The way I see it, you've got two options. One, you try to run and I shoot you. I say that because I will do it, and the cops around here, the Carabinieri, they won't care. They especially won't care when they find out what you're doing here. Your other option is to put on the handcuffs I give you, and head out to my car. I know you can't talk, but I've got a friend who has all kinds of ways that'll make you write down everything you know. And guess what, the doc's drugs are so good that you'll want to do it. Now how about that?"

Vespers didn't move. He wasn't planning on going anywhere with the black giant. While he hadn't heard of any drug that could make a man talk, let alone write a confession, something about the big man's demeanor told him that he was being told the truth.

Malik Vespers was a loyal employee. He had been while in the Secret Service, and now even more so under Cromwell. He owed the man his life. Vespers made his decision.

Pivoting on his right foot, he took off toward the far end of the infinity pool. He heard the shot and stumbled when the round hit him in the back. He could feel his legs starting to give, but he somehow kept them pumping. *Move. Move.* Another shot hit him in the shoulder but still he ran.

With a final leap, over the cliff he went, flying for the first time. Few thoughts crossed his mind as he fell toward the rocks below, some ten stories down. *Flying.* Then darkness.

MARINE MASTER SERGEANT Willy Trent looked over the ledge. The crushed form below wasn't moving. No way it would. Dude was deader than dead.

"Well, I guess that's option three," Trent said to the wind.

He pocketed Vespers's pistol and stuck his own in his back waist band. Gaucho was waiting out front in the tiny rented Fiat that he had a helluva time getting in and out of.

WALDO ERICKSON LOUNGED in the steaming water of his thermal bath. He'd paid a hefty sum to rent the private spa, telling the owner that he wanted 24-hour use of the place, and to be waited on hand and foot.

The owner had gladly taken the fat man's money. It would probably support his business for a year.

Beside Erickson lay an assortment of local delicacies. He ignored most, focusing on the delectable slices of grilled pizza, Neapolitan style. He preferred them simple with a light coat of olive oil and tomato sauce and a healthy heaping of buffalo mozzarella.

As he started in on his third pie, the oils from the sauce running down his chin as he shoved the whole piece in his mouth, he felt a tapping on his head.

He struggled to turn around as he chomped twice then swallowed the pizza whole. *It better not be the owner's daughter*, he thought. She knew better than to disturb him without calling out first.

It wasn't the owner's daughter. It was someone he'd never seen before. A younger guy. Brown hair. Good looking. Fit. He was wearing board shorts and a shirt like an American.

"Hey, look. I found Waldo," said the uninvited guest.

Erickson froze. He hadn't used his real name since they'd left the U.S.

"Who are you?"

The young man walked around the small bath and touched the rock walls like he was sightseeing.

"It doesn't matter who I am, Waldo. I've got a message for you."

Erickson could feel his bowels loosening. He didn't want to shit in the water. What did this guy want?

"Give me the message and then get the hell out of here,"

Erickson ordered, trying to regain a measure of dignity. He was used to control. Not this.

"I have a message from the president."

"What president?"

"The only one that matters, Waldo."

The young man walked back to stand behind Erickson.

"You tell Zimmer that if he tries to threaten me..."

"You mind if I have a piece of this pizza, Waldo?"

Erickson didn't know what to say. Who was this guy?

The guy shrugged, bent down, and picked up the remaining three quarters of the pizza. He folded it like you would a New York style pie, and took a big bite. His eyes closed as he savored Erickson's lunch.

"Wow. That's some good pizza," the man said through his mouthful of food.

"Would you *mind* getting to the point?"

The man swallowed and looked down at him.

"Here's the message. You crossed the line, Waldo. It's not okay to try to murder a whole race and then think you're gonna get away with it."

Erickson face paled despite the heat. "I don't know what you're—"

"Cut the crap, Waldo. You and Cromwell planned on killing every Arab on the planet. I get it that you're pissed about your brothers dying. Trust me, I'm a Marine. But this wasn't the way to do it."

"I didn't—"

Instead of answering, the young man pounced, bowling Erickson over in the water. He felt his face go under and tried to push the man off. He couldn't. Then, through it all, he felt the man shoving something into his mouth. He tried to clamp down but a finger did something to his jaw and his mouth opened involuntarily. Along with the bitter water he tasted the dough and the sauce of the pizza.

As Erickson began to lose consciousness, he wondered how they'd found him. He thought he'd been careful. And then his breath finally left him, and the murky blackness consumed him.

———

COL. GORMON CROMWELL was strapped to a chair when Cal arrived. Daniel was leaning against the wall, his arms across his chest, pistol in hand.

"Good afternoon," said Cal, running a hand through his still wet hair. "He give you any trouble?"

Daniel shook his head.

Cal pulled something out of his pocket. It was a syringe. Cromwell's eyes narrowed.

"I'll give you two guesses to see if you know what this is, Colonel."

"I know what it is and it won't work on me," said Cromwell, not the least bit of fear on his face. "If you're going to kill me just do it. I'd rather not sit here and listen to your bullshit threats."

Cal grinned. "You *think* you know what this is, but you're wrong. Want another guess?"

"No."

"Fine. I'll tell you. Did you know that your frog doctor was keeping a little insurance?"

By the slight widening of Cromwell's eyes, Cal saw that he hadn't known.

"He had a backup plan. And let me tell you what he made. This little sucker holds a specially made cocktail just for you. You see, Dr. Merrifield didn't trust you, Colonel. And people that don't trust you are bad news. This syringe contains a strain of the same stuff you were making, but it's mapped to your DNA. It's one of a kind. Just for you. Pretty cool, right?"

Cromwell just glared in response. Either he didn't care or he was trying to keep up his tough guy posture. Cal assumed the latter.

"So here we go. As a final thank you for all that you've done for our country, you get to be the first and last guinea pig for your sick as fuck project." Cal had moved closer and closer as he was talking and now stood directly beside the wannabe mass murderer. "Sorry, I don't have an alcohol swab."

Cal stabbed the exposed needle into the meat of Cromwell's thigh, depressing the plunger. Cromwell winced, but said nothing.

"Now, as it's been explained to me, this shit doesn't take long. You should probably be feeling the effects right about..."

Cromwell's body convulsed, the hyper energized cancer cells in his body feeding, expanding. The man's face contorted, the normal side bulging weirdly. He started to moan.

Cal took one last look at the man and left, Daniel right behind. Cromwell's dying wails followed them out to the car.

EPILOGUE

CHARLOTTESVILLE, VIRGINIA - 9:37AM, APRIL 22ND

Cal sat nursing a paper cup full of crushed ice and Famous Grouse. Someone had forgotten to do the dishes, and Cal was feeling lazy. It was a beautiful spring day, and they were headed to Foxfield in a couple hours. He hadn't been to the semi-annual horse races since he'd been a student at U.Va.

He thought about what they'd just accomplished. Not only had Neil and Jonas tracked Cromwell down through a building permit in Ischia, but Michael Thompson was back on U.S. soil. They'd found him on Erickson's swanky submarine, guarded by some dudes in silly white sailor outfits. When Cal, Daniel and thirteen others showed up at the dock, the crew was more than happy to let them board. The submarine was now property of the U.S. government, and Michael Thompson was back in school, cancer free and dealing with the fact that his father was a would-be mass murderer. The Senator would be locked up in maximum security isolation until the day he died. The number of people who knew where he was limited to a handful.

Dr. Merrifield was in the beginning stages of a very long debriefing, one that could very well last the duration of his Federal prison stay. Thanks to Dr. Higgins, the scientist was a virtual encyclopedia of nasty information. The guy was brilliant, but sick. Cal hoped they could use the research to help Dr. Price and prevent any similar occurrences in the future.

To add to the good news, Cal had just heard that Dr. Price's family business was back in working order. They'd managed to nab a couple lucrative government contracts thanks to President Zimmer. It was the least he could do to make up for the mix-up, and actually saved the government millions over the term of the contract. Not a bad deal for both sides.

Now that their first official mission was done, he felt that the boys deserved a day of boozin' it up and mingling with the pretty coeds who were always dressed in their spring finery.

Halfway into his early start, Cal closed his eyes and soaked in the sun's warmth on the back porch. Jonas had done a helluva job on the new patio, and they'd already made good use of the space. There was an unofficial gathering each night, and Top was all about grilling so they always had something great to eat. *I could get used to this.*

"Cal. You gonna get ready?" Neil was standing at the door, look splendiferous in a pair of blue and orange checkered pants and a nearly matching button-down shirt. A fellow U.Va alum, the sharp dressing Neil always had a new outfit for Foxfield.

"I'm coming. Chill out, grandpa."

Neil hated being late. Well, he hated being late to Foxfield. In day-to-day stuff Neil set his own 'on-time.' Today he wanted to be early, to really put on a tailgating spread that would woo the ladies. It was just his style.

"Don't make me take a paddle to ya, sonny!" Neil mocked, waving his hands over his head.

Cal laughed and got out of his chair. "You do the worst southern grandpappy impression that I've ever heard."

Neil gave him a middle finger along with a smug look and went back inside.

CAL WAS NOW DRESSED in what he thought was appropriate Foxfield attire, khaki shorts and a t-shirt that said, "I Almost Graduated."

The place was coming together, the living spaces now complete. Only the walls surrounding the compound were still under construction.

To cap it all off, they'd even come up with a name for their new venture. It had been Top's idea.

"I'm surprised you college guys haven't come up with it already. I think we should use Thomas Jefferson in the name. How about The Jefferson Group?"

"Why Jefferson?" Gaucho had asked.

"Jefferson was a bad dude, hombre. He gave the British Empire the finger by writing the Declaration of Independence. My favorite line he wrote was: 'We hold these truths to be self-evident, that all men are created equal, that they are endowed by their Creator with certain unalienable Rights, that among these are Life, Liberty and the pursuit of Happiness.' Isn't that what we've done from day one, protecting those rights?"

Top was right and the name stuck. *The Jefferson Group*. It sounded innocuous enough but had a meaning for the men who were part of the Charlottesville contingent.

Cal checked his laptop one more time, deleting a string of

emails that he didn't really care about. The last one caught his eye. It was an intelligence assessment regarding the further expansion of the Islamic State of Iraq and the Levant (ISIS) in Iraq. He clicked it open and was immediately greeted by the faces of the dead.

He read through the briefing, noting the tone of whoever had written it. Dispassionate, as if this wasn't happening to real people. It pissed Cal off. He clenched his hands into fists as he read on, furious by the end of the report.

But there wasn't anything he could do. He was one man with a small team. What the hell could they accomplish against a growing tide of 10,000? What could they do? What could *he* do?

The knock at the door shook Cal from his thoughts. "You coming?" asking Daniel, the only non-drinker and the designated driver for the day.

"Yeah. I'll be down in a minute."

Daniel left and Cal stood, thinking. He was torn. He'd done his time in Iraq. He'd often said that not even a command from God would make him go back. But now his thoughts changed. He felt a responsibility even if the rest of America didn't. While he was getting ready to drink and hang out with his friends, people were getting killed. No, not killed, they were being murdered.

Cal exhaled and picked up his cell phone. There was only one person he could think to call. That person picked up quickly.

"Brandon, I want to talk to you about what we can do in Iraq."

––––––

I hope you enjoyed this story.

If you did, please take a moment to write a review **ON AMAZON**. Even the short ones help!

GET A FREE COPY OF THE CORPS JUSTICE PREQUEL SHORT STORY, *GOD-SPEED*, JUST FOR SUBSCRIBING AT CG-COOPER.COM

ALSO BY C. G. COOPER

The Corps Justice Series In Order:

Back To War

Council Of Patriots

Prime Asset

Presidential Shift

National Burden

Lethal Misconduct

Moral Imperative

Disavowed

Chain Of Command

Papal Justice

The Zimmer Doctrine

Sabotage

Liberty Down

Sins Of The Father

Corps Justice Short Stories:

Chosen

God-Speed

Running

The Daniel Briggs Novels:

Adrift

Fallen

Broken

Tested

The Tom Greer Novels

A Life Worth Taking

The Spy In Residence Novels

What Lies Hidden

The Alex Knight Novels:

Breakout

The Stars & Spies Series:

Backdrop

The Patriot Protocol Series:

The Patriot Protocol

The Chronicles of Benjamin Dragon:

Benjamin Dragon – Awakening

Benjamin Dragon – Legacy

Benjamin Dragon - Genesis

ABOUT THE AUTHOR

C. G. Cooper is the *USA TODAY* and AMAZON BESTSELLING author of the CORPS JUSTICE novels (including spinoffs), The Chronicles of Benjamin Dragon and the Patriot Protocol series.

Cooper grew up in a Navy family and traveled from one Naval base to another as he fed his love of books and a fledgling desire to write.

Upon graduating from the University of Virginia with a degree in Foreign Affairs, Cooper was commissioned in the United States Marine Corps and went on to serve six years as an infantry officer. C. G. Cooper's final Marine duty station was in Nashville, Tennessee, where he fell in love with the laid-back lifestyle of Music City.

His first published novel, BACK TO WAR, came out of a need to link back to his time in the Marine Corps. That novel, written as a side project, spawned many follow-on novels, several exciting spinoffs, and catapulted Cooper's career.

Cooper lives just south of Nashville with his wife, three children, and their German shorthaired pointer, Liberty, who's become a popular character in the Corps Justice novels.

When he's not writing or hosting his podcast, Books In 30, Cooper spends time with his family, does his best to improve his golf handicap, and loves to shed light on the ongoing fight of everyday heroes.

Cooper loves hearing from readers and responds to every email personally.
To connect with C. G. Cooper visit
www.cg-cooper.com

64861723R00121

Made in the USA
Columbia, SC
12 July 2019